The Skating Rink

ALSO BY MILDRED LEE

The Rock and the Willow
Honor Sands

The Skating Rink

Mildred Lee

THE SEABURY PRESS
New York

Third Printing

Library of Congress Catalog Card Number: 69-13443

Printed in the United States of America.

To James Giblin

1

IT WAS early September and still hot when Pete Degley began to build his roller-skating rink. The site was a piece of land between the highway and the scraggly peach orchard that belonged to Tuck Faraday's father, Myron. Somehow, Tuck's father never got around to spraying the trees, so the fruit was too poor to market and Tuck's stepmother, Ida, grumblingly put it up for the family's use.

Nearing the end of his long walk from school, Tuck saw the bright yellow Chevy and a couple of trucks standing on the shoulder of the highway. He was staring from under the ragged hair hanging over his forehead when the man sauntered up and spoke to him. He was a short, wiry, tough-looking little man with a brown, seamed face and bright, hot eyes that looked as if little fires burned behind them.

"Degley's the name," he said. "Pete Degley." His handshake made Tuck feel older than his fifteen years and he liked the feeling. Pete Degley told Tuck he was going to put a roller-skating rink here beside the highway, confiding in him so naturally that it wasn't till afterwards, when he thought the whole thing over, that Tuck saw anything unusual about it.

"Know how come me to pick out this spot?" The man adjusted his yellowed Panama hat so that it rode jauntily on the back of his head. "It's pretty near equal distance from Fidelia, Cantrell, Enfield, *and* Magnolia. Not one of those towns has got a rink—not even Magnolia that, being as big a place as it is, you would think might have one." He paused as if to allow Tuck to be properly impressed. Tuck was. "You from around here, son?"

Tuck nodded, not minding that Pete Degley had called him son. It didn't cut him down to size after the manly handshake; it made him feel included and liked.

"Whereabouts?"

Sweat broke out on Tuck's upper lip that he'd been shaving, unknown to his father, a month or more. The necessity to speak had overtaken him and he was not ready. He pointed to the huddle of outbuildings, the long chicken house and the dwelling of sagged gray clapboards above and beyond the peach orchard. "Up-Up y-yonder, sir."

Pete Degley cut a twig from a stunted persimmon tree with his pocketknife and whittled it to toothpick size. "I don't believe I got your name," he said, as if he hadn't noticed Tuck's stammering.

Tuck flipped his science notebook open and held it so close the man had to step back and squint at the name written with a fine flourish in green ink. He read it aloud, lingeringly, as if it pleased him: "Tucker Holland Faraday." He chewed his toothpick, his brow creased in thought, then shook his head. "I don't believe I've happened to run acrost any Faradays around here. Or anywheres else I've been, and that covers considerable territory if I do say so myself." He grinned at Tuck, showing teeth that looked white and strong—all but two front ones that were faintly discolored. "It's a fine-sounding name, though. Faraday." And he looked dreamily toward the tops of the peach trees, shifting his toothpick slowly from one side of his slightly crooked mouth to the other.

One of the surveyors came up with a question and Pete Degley excused himself courteously and walked away with him. Tuck stood for a moment, looking after them, questions of his own rising to fill his mind. How long would it take to build a roller rink? How big would it be? What would it cost to skate in it—if you could skate? Did anybody else know about it, or had this Mr. Pete Degley, for some reason of his own, discussed his business only with Tuck? The last was so foolish it made Tuck blush as he turned away, glancing out of the sides of his eyes at Pete Degley and the surveyors, and started up through the orchard by a path no one but he ever used.

He had just ducked under the fringe of trees when Pete Degley's shout made him turn.

"So long, Faraday. See you around."

Tuck waved, bashful because of the surveyors' watching eyes. He hurried along the uneven path, his breath coming faster than the slight rise warranted. He was about halfway through the orchard when it struck him that today was special. Two things had happened. He had made up his mind to quit school and he had met Pete Degley.

His decision had occurred suddenly this time, brought on by Elva Grimes's laughing at him in the classroom. Miss Bayliss, Tuck's English teacher, had asked a question that had fallen into the boredom and indifference of the class like a rock rolling into a dry creek bed. Tuck knew the answer and had raised his hand—a thing he never did. He couldn't imagine why he had done it this time unless Elva's smile across the aisle at him a moment before the question had rattled him out of his senses. Anyway, he had started, fool-like, to answer, halting and stammering under the greedily curious eyes of the class.

Then Elva had giggled, a high, thin giggle that started the others and confused Tuck so badly he hadn't even got the answer out—couldn't have, even if it hadn't left his head by then. Bent over his desk, hot and hating himself and Elva and everybody in the room, with Miss Bayliss angrily calling the class to order, he had made his decision to quit school. This time it would stand. It could because he would be sixteen, come March. He would quit then and nobody could do a thing about it.

It wouldn't be like the other times he'd quit—letters from the truant officer, tears from his stepmother, beatings from his father. He was too big for a licking now—a good two inches taller than his father—and he thought the old man might be glad not to have to buy shoes for him so often. Walking the two miles from the Faraday farm to the big new high school in Wesley was hard on shoes, especially cheap ones. It wore them out in a hurry.

"How come you've got to walk it when I pay taxes for a bus to carry you?" Myron Faraday had said in the beginning, anger gathering like a cloud in his face that shrank in upon its bones a little more with each year's petty failures. "Looks like you just can't stand it to act like ever'-body else. Got to be different—like you was tetched." The last words were soaked in bitterness.

And his half sister Karen had said, softly, "I know why Tuck don't want to ride the bus." Her pale eyes had smiled at him with a hint of slyness. "The kids pick on him and mock him. They call him Dummy." The pink tip of her tongue slid over her lips, tasting the word she was forbidden by her mother to use.

"I didn't hear anybody ask your opinion, miss," Tuck's stepmother had said then, sharpness taking the customary whine out of her voice. Ida was good about taking up for Tuck, but he wished she wouldn't. It emphasized his need for defense, a need he despised and wanted to deny to himself.

It was true that the kids on the bus heckled him, mimicking his stammer if he spoke, calling him Dummy when he resorted to stubborn silence, as he did more and more. One year there had been a lady driver. She had yelled at the kids to shut up or she'd turn every last one of them in to the Principal. But she'd only made matters worse, insisting that Tuck sit up front with the first-graders and second-graders. That was when he'd started walking, though it meant getting up an hour earlier to get his chores done, without any help from his brothers Tom and Cletus.

Tuck came out of the orchard into the untidy yard,

his nostrils twitching at the scent drifting from the long chicken house perched on the ridge above the cut-over corn patch behind the Faraday house. It was the only time he noticed the smell; when he quit school, he thought, he wouldn't notice it at all. The meeting with Pete Degley had made him late and he expected his father's anger. Tuck didn't care. He had long since learned to lock himself into his silence and wait there, with a feeling almost of safety, for the verbal storm to pass.

He picked his way through the familiar litter of the yard to the back door. As he set his foot on the step he paused, hearing his father's voice, loud with anger, in the kitchen and his stepmother's plaintive whine in answer.

". . . late again," his father was saying. "No sense in him walking when he could ride. He's stubborn as a mule. Like not talking if he don't want to. He talked good as anybody before his mama was drowned—and him only three years old then. Now, you could beat him half to death and he'd just clam up tighter'n ever."

"I was you, I'd just leave him alone," his stepmother said. Through the open window Tuck could hear the thump of her iron. "Younguns go through diff'rent stages. You ask me, Tuck's a better hand at mighty near ever'thing he does around here than them twins, I don't care who you're partial to. Tom will lie you black in the face and Clete would sass the First Lady if she was to get in his road. I declare I never seen such a boy to smart off."

"Well, you're not likely to get any sass from Tuck," the father threw out, and Tuck felt his armor of silence pierced by the bitterness in his father's tone.

He went through the kitchen, not speaking. In the room he shared with the twins, Tom and Cletus, he quickly changed his school clothes for work shirt and blue jeans. The slap of the back screen door announced his father's going out, and from the front of the house the voices of Karen's TV movie came through the thin walls with soulful intensity.

While Tuck worked with his father, putting feed in the troughs for the chickens, filling the water fountains, mending a loose board in the chicken house wall, he thought of the time when he would be out of school. March was a long way off, but it would come. The days would gnaw at the weeks and months till they were consumed—bright fall and dull winter and then, with the coming of spring, Tuck would be sixteen. He would cast the burden of school and its long, teasing pain from him.

He felt almost happy contemplating it. Maybe his father would be pleased, too. He was always complaining that he was shorthanded, a complaint Cletus and Tom, the twin brothers, ignored. Though far from scholarly, they preferred school to work on the chicken farm. And they had made it clear they intended to find jobs elsewhere when they graduated from Wesley High next June. Meanwhile, they picked up occasional work in Wesley and spent most of their spare time at the Mayhew farm, less than a quarter of a mile from home, contesting amiably for Tolly Mayhew's favor.

Tuck had a sneaking hope that if he became his father's right-hand man there might be less friction between them. He jumped as Myron spoke.

"I was aiming to start on that piece of roof next week, but I ain't going to get to it."

Tuck wanted to say, "We'll patch it up till spring, Pa. Then I'll be here to help you fix it right." But he was silent, taking a nail from between his lips, turning the hammer in his hand.

"A man can't get to ever'thing by hisself." Wrath made Myron's voice loud.

"N-No, sir," Tuck said and seemed to feel his father's anger subsiding as he sloshed water in a bucket, rinsing it. He knew his silences enraged Myron—but so many things did. Tuck had no way of gauging the deeper causes. Sometimes, it seemed to him that his existence was one of them. Now that he was man-sized, he scorned the thought. It was kid stuff—like wishing his father would come in to him when he used to have that dream that made him cry out in his sleep.

In the dream he was always standing on the shore of the pond and his mother was out there in the water that kept rising with terrible swiftness. Her long hair hung, slimy, round her neck and over her breast and Tuck would be trying to call out, but no sound would come except the slop of muddy waves at his feet. Though he was mute in the nightmare he would yell loud enough, actually, to bring his stepmother, stumbling and bleary-eyed with sleep, to his bedside. Even then Tuck had known it was a woman's job to soothe a frightened child in the night. But he'd always wished anyhow that his father would wake and come to him. Even if he was angry at having his rest disturbed. If he would come, just once, and maybe touch Tuck and say,

"There now" or "It was just a bad old dream"—or anything at all. But he never did. It was always Ida. And before her, Tuck's Aunt Cleo, Myron's widowed sister who kept house for him till he married Ida.

Tuck banged a nail into the loose board so hard the wall of the chicken house quivered. Karen's head, ridged with rows of pink plastic rollers, appeared at the wire-covered opening. She twined her fat fingers round the wire netting and grinned at Tuck. He sat back on his lean haunches and stared straight at her. She stared back, her pale-lashed eyes defiant, but Tuck knew he could win, he always did. He had only to keep it up and her lids would flicker, then her gaze would slide away, intimidated by his cold, persistent stare.

Sometimes, just for the heck of it, Tuck varied the process. He would lift his lips like a snarling dog till a line of gum showed above his square, white teeth. Or he would make a gargling sound deep in his throat and Karen would run, shrieking, to be folded against the maternal breast, or scolded, depending upon the mood of her mother.

Today, hammer in hand, Tuck simply kept his still gray eyes upon her. Before her eyes more than flinched Karen said on a breathless giggle, "I know somebody that likes you, Tuck. A girl! It's Elva Grimes."

Tuck's stare did not swerve as his heart gave a sick lurch and settled into a heavy thudding. He wasn't the only one, then, who had seen Elva Grimes looking at him out of the sides of her eyes and whispering with her head close to the head of that Foster girl she ran with. He could hear again her thin, high giggle in English class, hear it as plainly as the tormenting singsong Karen began: "Tucker's got a gur-rl, Tuck has got a gur-rl."

He wanted to yell, "Get your stupid head full of pink sewer pipes out of that window before I take this hammer to it." But he did not part his lips, knowing Karen would be inside the house before he could get half the words out. Besides, it was beneath his dignity. He was man-sized and it was time he acted his age. He tried to tell himself this bratty kid's teasing was no more than a mosquito you slapped at in the dark of a summer night. But some of his fury must have communicated itself to Karen, for she unlatched her fingers from the wire mesh and backed off.

Walking backwards, stumbling over the corn stubble, she called, "Linny Foster told me, and her sister Mimi is Elva's best girl friend." She turned and bolted toward the house.

"You scaring your sister again?" Tuck's father said behind him. His flat voice, speaking from habit, showed no real concern. Tuck looked over his shoulder, pressed his lips tighter together. "She wouldn't aggravate you so much if you was to speak up and answer her back like Tom or Clete would. Like you'd ought to. You ever think of that?"

Tuck drove another nail into the board, though it wasn't needed. The pounding eased him, draining off some of his anger. He puttered about the chicken house, giving himself time to simmer down to normal. Going slowly toward the house at last, he was able to call the image of the man Pete Degley to his mind. The slow, yet energetic walk, the knotty brown hands, generous with gestures filled with meaning, the quick brown eyes with those little hot fires behind them.

Again the inexplicable tingle of excitement gripped Tuck, a feeling of something about to happen. He couldn't imagine what; running into a strange guy was nothing to get shook up over, but the man Degley was not like anyone else. Some force had seemed to come from him, to rub off on Tuck, giving him that feeling of expectancy. Maybe it didn't make sense but it was new and powerful enough to scatter his thoughts of Elva Grimes and his old, childish longing for his father's friendliness.

Karen's head came cautiously round the corner of the house. Under the plastic rollers her plump cheeks were creased with fearful anticipation. Tuck knew she expected him to at least make one of his worst faces at her, but he didn't give her the satisfaction.

2

THE NEXT DAY, when Tuck came from school, a great pile of concrete blocks lay where the rink was going to be and a truck was turning off the highway with another load. Tuck looked eagerly about for Pete Degley but did not see him. The yellow Chevrolet was not there, either. After standing around a few moments, watching the unloading of the blocks, he went slowly to the house.

That night talk buzzed round the supper table.

"Whatever are they fixing to build down yonder?" Ida wondered, pushing a tag of hair off her cheek and tucking it behind her ear.

"Might could be a motel," Cletus guessed, rounding black-eyed peas up with a scrap of corn bread.

"Aw, that's not going to be no motel," Tom objected; it was a matter of principle for the twins to disagree. "It's not nowheres big enough. Not the right kind of material. Might could be a beer joint."

"A beer joint!" Ida Faraday shook her head so vigorously the lock of hair escaped from behind her ear and dangled over her plate again. "Oh, goodness me, I do hope not."

Myron Faraday cleared his throat. "I'd of known anybody wanted land down there I could of sold them that old orchard. Reckon didn't anybody want to bulldoze the trees down. Folks just gets sorrier and no-accounter ever' day, looks like."

Tom and Clete exchanged looks. No one looked at Tuck. It was one of the times when his silence seemed to render him invisible to those about him. His secret knowledge gave him a feeling of superiority that was rare and exciting.

Construction on the rink began and Tuck spent as much time as he could on the site. So long as he was not too late getting home and did the work required of him, no one showed any interest in his solitary pursuits. Every detail of the job fascinated him. He began to think it wouldn't be bad to be a carpenter or a mason. Driving the concrete mixer wasn't to be sneezed at, either. What a feeling it must give a builder to watch something like this roller rink taking shape under his hands!

Tuck grudged the hours he had to spend in school, so much happened from one afternoon to the next. He covered the two miles in such haste that he always arrived at the site breathless and sweaty, making the most of the few minutes he could allow himself without rousing his father's temper. His excitement heightened as the building took shape, looming like an enormous Quonset hut with big Miami windows and a floor as smooth as glass.

As September flowed into October with a brightening and browning of leaves, word got around that a roller rink was going up beside the highway. Tuck was sorry; he had liked hugging the knowledge to himself in his silence. His interest in the man, Pete Degley, grew, intensified by the fact that knowledge of the rink was no longer his alone. He found himself talking to Pete, hesitating and stammering dreadfully in the beginning, his skin moist and his fists driven desperately into his pockets. But Pete Degley paid no attention to Tuck's difficulty, never interrupting to help him along as people tended to do, giving the appearance of having all the time in the world to let him finish what he started to say. The man's calm acceptance of him as he was gradually eased the tensions in Tuck, encouraged him to venture further out of his silence as the days slipped by, golden and warm and touched with a strange, new peace that could be quickly shattered and was the more precious for that.

There was the Saturday morning when, after his chores, Tuck slipped down to the rink and Pete Degley asked, out of the blue and startling him, "You ever play basketball?"

"N-N-No, sir."

They were sitting on a board across two sawhorses. Pete was whittling. He whittled a lot—cutting toothpicks, turning out crude bits of carving, paring a thin stick to delicate, curled shavings he pushed at with the toe of a highly polished brown shoe. He set great store by his pocketknife, Pete Degley did, like a kid. Yet, somehow, nothing he did was childish. His hands were at home on his knife, making it a part of him.

"You look to me like a good build for a basketball player." His bright eyes traveled the length of Tuck's form. "Good heighth. Limber joints. Good, long legs with plenty but not too much of 'em turned up for feet." He turned back to his whittling, a soft grin on his tough face. Tuck could see a little rooster shaping under the clever brown fingers. "Don't take to school exactly, do you." Tuck didn't feel it was a question and said nothing.

Pete Degley tossed the bit of wood aside and Tuck, with a quick, half-embarrassed motion, retrieved it and put it in his pocket. Maybe he would give it to Karen—and maybe he would keep it. He watched Pete fold his knife and slip it into his pocket. Nearby, the scrape-scrape of a trowel spreading mortar on rough block grated in the bright autumn air.

Tuck wanted suddenly to open up and spill the long, weighted misery of his school days—all the taunts and jeers, the sniggering that had merged and swollen into the monstrous wound he had resolved to endure no longer than the law made necessary. He could bear them at home. There he was known, an accustomed part of the family, accepted, however gracelessly, as one of them. He belonged—at least, they thought he did. But at school each time he opened his mouth and permitted his crippled words to jerk and stumble forth it was like a first time.

There had been exceptions. He would have liked to tell Pete Degley about the little girl, Lucie, back in the fifth grade when the Faradays lived between Cleveland and Gainesville and Tuck's father had the sawmill there. Laurel Gap it was called, a wide place in the road in sight of the Blue Ridge Mountains. It had a post office, a general store and a lumber yard and Tuck's father's sawmill.

Tuck had not thought of Lucie in years, but that bright Saturday morning, sitting there with Pete Degley, her pointed face and big eyes the color of branch water with the sun on it came clear as yesterday in his mind. He had never let himself think about her because what happened left a bitter taste, so he had spat it out of his mind. It came back, that morning, bitter taste and all.

He had risked a licking and gone home with Lucie one day. He had showed her how to play mumblety-peg. They sat on the bottom step of Lucie's front porch, flipping Tuck's pocketknife into the clay soil. In a moment between their laughter and shrill voices Lucie's mother had said to a neighbor in the porch swing, not quite low enough, "Why, she's even beginning to pick up his stutter. I don't know what to do. I feel real sorry for the boy, but—" And the neighbor woman had cut in: "After all, you've got your own child to think of."

Chill with the memory, Tuck reckoned he didn't want to tell Mr. Degley that.

Then, there was Link Grover in Wesley. Link was good-looking and popular with both girls and boys. He played football for Junior Varsity, but he wasn't good at his schoolwork. Tuck, who would never answer a question orally in school, but always got good grades on his written work, had done Link's English themes and book reports all last year and kept his science notebook up to date for him. Link never made fun of Tuck and never avoided him, but once—only once—Tuck had seen Link redden and look down when some of the other guys did. After that, somehow, the friendship wasn't much good, and Tuck kept out of Link's way.

He didn't tell Mr. Degley that, either.

"I-I'm going to quit school, Mr. D-Degley," Tuck blurted. "S-Soon as I'm s-sixteen."

"Mmmmm. Well. I reckon you know your own mind best," Pete Degley said, nibbling thoughtfully at his toothpick. "A guy—one like you, anyhow—wouldn't just settle on a thing like that without studying on it a good bit. You strike me as a bright young fellow, not one to do something rash and foolish for no good reason." He pushed at the shavings with his toe. "Way it is today, a man can't hardly make a living without he's got some education. A young feller that is, just starting out." He pushed the felt hat that had replaced the yellowed panama to the back of his head and rubbed at the thinning hair above his forehead. "Looks like he's got nothing to latch onto."

All that day Tuck kept remembering that Mr. Degley had called him a "bright young fellow." It made a sort of groove in his mind that he kept going over and over. He scoffed at himself for making such a thing of it; it was just Mr. Degley's way of talking. Or maybe he felt sorry for Tuck on account of the trouble he had with words. But Tuck couldn't buy that. Pete Degley wasn't one to say what he didn't mean.

There was something he hadn't thought of, sitting

there in the sun with Mr. Degley—something that happened his first year in Wesley school. Funny it hadn't come back to him along with those other things. Maybe he had buried it a little deeper than Lucie. At any rate, it wasn't till he had left Pete Degley and was going home that Miss Eggers popped into his mind like a rabbit out of a thicket.

Miss Eggers was his English teacher that first year. Tuck reckoned she liked him because he was quiet and didn't smart off in class like the other boys. She tried, as embarrassed as Tuck, to persuade him to talk. Not in class, with the other kids sure to mock him every chance they got, but afterwards, going over his written work with him. That is, she thought she was with him but she wasn't; Tuck would shut the door of his mind and let her struggle along by herself. She was a teacher, wasn't she? Teachers had never been on Tuck's side. And she was a woman, which made it too much like his stepmother taking up for him.

"You've got a good mind, Tucker," Miss Eggers had said. "If you would only forget this—this little flaw in your speech. Everyone has imperfections. Sometimes they even help."

She told him about a man, then, who lived way back nearly four hundred years before Christ. His name was Demosthenes. Tuck had thought sure she was going to make him try to say Demosthenes and he started feeling mulish—like when his father jumped all over him for not answering.

Miss Eggers didn't do that. She told him this Demosthenes was a Greek, one of the greatest orators of all time. "Do you know what he did, Tucker, to make his speech more perfect?" Tuck had looked at her, curious in spite of himself, and Miss Eggers said, "He put pebbles in his mouth and practiced speaking round them."

Tuck had thought, The pore dumb ox. He must've been a fool for punishment, sure enough, toting around a mouthful of rocks! Just for a moment he had wished Tom and Clete were there to hear that one—

"You see, there was a person with a great gift, destined for fame, who thought an obstacle would help him perfect what he wanted to do." She looked shiny-eyed, eager as a kid about to bite into an ice cream cone. Pink came up into her cheeks. "I'm not a speech therapist, Tucker. But I might be able to help you—if you'd let me. A few minutes after school two or three afternoons a week—"

Tuck had told her he had to catch the bus, knowing she knew that pupils who rode the bus weren't kept in after school. The next year he stopped riding the bus, but Miss Eggers wasn't at the Wesley school then. She'd married somebody in Enfield and Tuck never saw her again. Anyhow, he hadn't been about to sit in a classroom with a little old girl of a teacher, saying words after her like a parrot.

Just for a little while, though, he had come close to taking an interest in school. Miss Eggers had written that crazy Greek's name on the margin of his paper and Tuck had put the darn thing under the wrapping paper Ida lined the bureau drawers with and forgotten it till this morning. Remembering it wasn't going to make any more difference than Mr. Degley's calling him bright. He was quitting school in March and the heck with it.

That night, sitting in the kitchen with the family, Tuck had a curious experience. He saw the family as if he had been away for a long time. Maybe it was just that he seldom really looked at them. Why he should want to now he didn't know. Darkness had brought a sudden, sharp cold and the wood-burning range threw remnants of heat from supper's fire into the kitchen, holding them for a little while from their separate pursuits.

Ida looked up from the mending in her lap with a sigh. "Keeps up like this, My, you'll have to set up the heating stove." Myron didn't reply and she went on, plaintively, "I always hate to start it, smelling up the whole house with kerosene. What in the world do you do to your pockets, Tuck Faraday? I vow, anybody'd think you was loaded with loose change, the linings tore out thisaway."

"Maybe he is," Tom said and Cletus observed, slyly, "Could be old Tuck gets paid for helping shove a rock outa the way ever' now and then down yonder at the roller rink. What you and that dark-complected guy find to talk about so much, anyhow?" He winked at Ida. "You wouldn't know our quiet boy, Ma, see him with that feller—looks like some kind of a foreigner to me—that's putting up the rink. Tuck's dern near gabby, I swear." He slapped his knee and cackled, joined by his twin brother.

"You-uns don't watch out, you'll like to die laughing," Ida remarked, tartly. "If Tuck could pick him up a job somewheres I'd say it was to his credit."

Tuck felt a twinge of the old guilt at his failure to appreciate his stepmother's taking up for him. He had always felt that she shared the belief of those who thought him not quite right in his head. It made him prefer his father's rage and his brothers' taunting. Even as a child, he'd never been able to meet her feeble attempts at mothering halfway. He looked at her, though, bent over his pants. He looked at her rounded back, her limp tags of hair, her eyes squinted at the stitches because she needed new glasses that cost money.

He looked at Cletus who was tilted back against the wall in the kitchen chair, his legs sprawled, eyes half-closed, the ragged hair on his neck dyed the bright yellow some of the Wesley High boys went in for. In Tom, Tuck's glance found almost an echo of Cletus, but with a slackness about mouth and chin he had never noticed before. His eyes traveled to Karen, a chubby little kid breathing through her mouth as she struggled with arithmetic at the kitchen table.

Tuck's look went slowly to his father's face. Almost fleshless, sharp and leathery and bitter, it confronted Tuck, old beyond its years, though Tuck did not know the number of his father's years, had never thought about it before. He only knew it pained him, somehow laid an obligation on him, to see his father's face so. If he could speak out for once with a gift of gab to equal his brothers' and tell his father and the others what he and Pete Degley talked about, would their faces change at all—or stay the same?

Ida twitched the trousers right side out, shook them, and hung them on the back of a chair. "You'd stop shoving your paws so hard in your pockets, they might not bust on you like that." She yawned rendingly, her eyes watering, and rubbed her stout, bare arms. "Feels kinda chilly in here, now. I wouldn't be surprised if it come on to a early frost." She laid a hand on Karen's neck where the hair divided and fell in taffy-colored tails across her chest. "Put your stuff away, doll, and get to bed. You got your feet to wash yet, and you're going to be mighty sleepy in the morning."

Tom and Clete went down the hall and out the front door.

"Going to Mayhews', I reckon, late as it is," Ida grumbled, her eyes flicking past Tuck to his father's empty chair.

It was Myron Faraday's custom to make a nightly pilgrimage round the place, checking the safety of his chickens, the milk cow, the two hogs. He would not keep a watch dog. Mr. Buddy Mayhew had given Tuck a hound puppy when the Faradays first came to the farm, but it grew up to have a fondness for raw eggs and, after two crimes of egg-sucking, Tuck's father had shot it.

Tuck stayed on in the kitchen after the others had gone to bed. He thought fleetingly of his books on the hall table where he had left them when he came in, yesterday. Then he shrugged; since he had made up his mind to drop out of school it seemed silly to do homework if he wasn't in the mood. He thought about digging that old English paper out of the drawer and reading it—the one with the Greek's name spelled out in the margin. No. Not tonight. He wanted just to sit here by himself and think about things Pete Degley had said to him at one time and another. He wished he hadn't remembered that seventh-grade teacher, Miss Eggers.

3

THE DAY was sunny, not cold, but with a nip in the air that made brisk walking a pleasure and with a blue sky arching gaily overhead.

Tuck had discovered a shortcut out of town that saved him all of ten minutes on the walk home. Ten minutes he could spend at the rink site. It gave him a personal satisfaction to check on the day's progress—and there was always the chance of seeing Pete Degley.

The shorter way lay through an old, shabby part of Wesley. The houses were far apart, two or three of them vacant with For Sale signs standing tipsily in their weedy yards. There was nothing to prevent Tuck's going through these sad old properties, so he was able to save himself a good many steps and a few more minutes.

He was cutting across the yard of the old Harper house that had burned down and never been replaced when he heard his name called softly. He looked round him, not quite believing his ears, and the call came again, a little louder. There, a few feet away, behind a big banana shrub, was Elva Grimes's yellow head and a patch of green sweater.

It was the first time Tuck had ever seen her without Mimi Foster. He looked sharply, expecting the other girl to materialize somehow, but she didn't. There was only Elva Grimes, parting the branches of the shrub so that more of her face was visible. She was looking at him the way girls looked at boys, neither shyly nor boldly, yet a little of both and with something else for which Tuck had no name. He had seen Tolly Mayhew look at his brothers like that—sometimes one, sometimes the other, and not infrequently at both Tom and Clete at the same time.

Tuck's impulse was to walk on as if he hadn't heard, but he knew it was too late for that. He was hooked and he'd have to face her down and see it through, one way or another. He stood still, shifting his books from one arm to the other, and seemed to hear his half sister's teasing singsong in the chicken yard, "Tucker's got a gur-rl . . ."

Elva said, "Hi, Tuck," and came from behind the shrub, looking quickly and cautiously around, the heavy hair sliding on her shoulders. It was the yellow of corn tassels before they turn brown and as the sunlight struck across it, it gleamed like gold. "Have you got a minute?" she said, her voice catching in a way that made Tuck's chest tighten. "I want to talk to you."

He noticed her arms, round and white, under the pushed-up sweater sleeves and they had pale gold freckles on them like those on her face. She smiled. "Want me to walk a piece of the way with you?" She looked down and Tuck saw her eyelids, white and heavy. He wanted suddenly to touch them, to see if they were as smooth and soft as they looked. He had never had that tingle in his fingers before; it frightened him, he didn't know why.

He made a motion to go on his way, but Elva drew herself up, making herself as tall as she could, which wasn't very tall, and twisted her body the way girls at Wesley High did when they knew a boy was looking.

"Tuck! Don't you want me to walk with you?"

He looked down at her pouting smile and shook his head. Let her think about the way she'd made fun of him in English class not long ago. What was Elva Grimes, or any other girl, to him, anyhow?

"Aw, why don't you, Tucker?" She touched his arm and the touch ran through his body like an electric shock. He looked up and down the street as she had a moment before. Not a living soul in sight; all the houses had a blind and empty look. It was as if he and Elva Grimes were alone in the world together. The muscles of his throat began to ache and he could not bear to look at her.

He started to walk, hearing in befuddled wonder her flat-heeled green shoes trotting along beside his shabby ones. Elva chattered happily—as if he had been Tom or Clete or Link Grover. She held her round little chin high and her eyes were bright. She was like a bird, Tuck thought, an unfamiliar tenderness drifting through his excitement and fear. He wished they could walk on indefinitely while he got used to the new feelings both pleasing and bewildering him.

The lonely street petered out into a country lane that wound down toward the creek. It was part of Tuck's shorter way home. He glanced at Elva to see if she would stop and turn back. She did not hesitate, but went with him down the lane. The woods were cool and dim after the sunny street and Elva shivered enchantingly, squeezing her arms across her round breasts.

Tuck motioned to a low mound covered with pine needles. Still, Elva did not hesitate. She sat down and prettily arranged her skirt. Her little woman ways delighted him, as the child Lucie had, long ago. There was a child's ring on her finger and dimples across the backs of her hands. Her corn-colored hair moved lazily across her neck and when he sat down beside her its fragrance teased his nostrils.

"Talk to me, Tuck," Elva said, laughter—not ridiculing, friendly and gentle—beneath her words.

A sweet and terrible fire throbbed through Tuck as he laid his books down and moved timidly nearer her. She did not draw away and he felt the warmth of her nearness like the fire in him.

"Talk to me," she said again and turned her face toward him, her lips parted. "You haven't said a single word all this time. It's like I'm talking to myself!" He could feel her breath against his wrist as he tremblingly touched her hair. His world of fear and caution and animal alertness vanished, consumed by the sweet, strange fire. He thought that if he could touch her he could communicate, maybe even speak to her without shame. Through a mist he saw her hands, one lying on the other, in her lap. The green stone in her little ring caught the light sifting through pine branches. He put his hand over the ring, cupping it in warm darkness. He laid his cheek against hers, marveling at its softness, and she was silent as he, and motionless.

Tuck could scarcely breathe for the longing that filled him with both a trembling joy and an unbearable ache. Without his intending it to, with only the longing and joy in him, his mouth moved gently across her cheek, seeking her lips.

The shock of her hand across the side of his head sent him sprawling backward, his ear stinging from the cut of her child ring. His eyes swam, came slowly to focus on her quivering upright figure. He saw her eyes, glazed with fear and shame, and thought with brief and bitter grief that he had not touched the lids. He could not believe what had happened; only his humiliation was real as he picked himself up and brushed at his clothes. A few pine needles fell, shimmering, from his good school pants. A trickle of blood crept from his ear down his neck.

"Dummy," Elva shrilled. "You big dumb dope, you! I thought you could talk. I told my girl friend—I told Mimi I'd make you talk. I had a bet with her. I could of done it, too, if you had the sense to. I can make boys do anything I want! But you haven't got good sense. You're like they said. All you can do is be fresh—because you don't have to talk to do that. You won't ever have a nice girl or nothing else. You're a dummy, a dummy, a dummy!"

She whirled and pounded through the bit of pine woods toward the lane, her choked sobs dying as the distance swallowed her.

Tuck stood perfectly still on the mound, not thinking,

not feeling. He didn't know whether it was seconds or minutes. He heard, as if he were someone else, the whisper of the pine needles, the cheeky note of a bird he couldn't see, the chuckle of the creek beyond a wild plum thicket.

Slowly, cautiously, as though crawling into his own skin again, he collected himself, wiped the blood from his neck lest it soil his shirt. He gathered his books and walked the long way home. He would not let himself think of what had happened. If he never thought of it, it would cease to be. Like Lucie and his nightmare of the pond.

There was no sign of Pete Degley's car at the rink; the workmen were preparing to go. The afternoons had begun to draw in and Tuck felt lateness in the chill air on his face, saw it in the red of the sun slipping to the horizon. His old man would be all over him. So what. He couldn't care less. With a raised hand, a jerk of the head, he saluted the workman locking the tool shed.

Before he was out of the orchard Tuck heard his brothers' voices in the chicken yard. Let them do his chores for once, Tuck thought, he'd done theirs many a time. He felt completely insulated by indifference to his father's anger.

A glance at his stepmother showed Tuck she had been crying. Her thickened lids and pink nose did not make her any prettier. She bent to fiddle with the stove door and a rusty bolt dropped out of it and rolled under the stove. Ida Faraday landed a furious kick in the middle of the oven door, rattling the clumsy old stove and wincing at bruised toes.

"Wood stove!" she yelled. "I bet you could load ever' one there is left in the county—ever' one in the state of Georgia—in the trunk of a car an' have room for a crate of chickens besides! I want me a 'lectric stove so bad, looks like I purely can't stand it sometimes."

Tuck picked the bolt from under the stove, glanced at it and threw it into the wood box. The door of the fire box hung on its one sound hinge, cracks of orange light outlining it. He went to the tool shed, a lean-to off the kitchen, and brought out a cigar box full of salvaged screws, bolts, nails, and tacks. With a hammer and screwdriver he repaired the door, blistering a finger in the process and cursing under his breath.

"Well, I guess it'll get supper cooked without I burn the house down," Ida muttered by way of thanks.

Tuck looked out into the yard that was graying with twilight and decided to make a show of doing homework. He spread his books and papers on the table. The act seemed to unloose talk long dammed within his stepmother. The monotonous rise and fall of her voice beat against his ears as he copied some random notes he had scribbled in school.

"Reckon you must take after your mama, Tuck. You got her looks, too—only I guess I ought to say you got her daddy's looks. You do favor old man Holland a right smart, now you've run up so tall." She poured buttermilk into her wooden bread bowl and with pudgy, work-roughed fingers mixed flour and lard into it. "Law me. The ruckus them Hollands made when your mama run off and married your daddy. They like to died off right then. But there's no accounting for the notions a teen-age girl may get into her head. Don't you never get married till you're a man grown, Tuck."

Tuck's pen stopped in the middle of a word. Married. Him. He saw Elva Grimes's eyelids, thick and white as a magnolia petal, and his throat felt scalded. He tightened his fingers on the pen, pushing it to complete the word. Writing with his stepmother running off at the mouth was something like talking, he thought, jabbing the period through the paper.

"Your mama was just a little old youngun, didn't know nothing but town things," Ida droned on like the buzzing of a summer fly. "Your papa didn't show good sense, being a heap older than her, neither. By rights he should of knowed nothing but misfortune would come out of it. Them Hollands thought theirselves better than country folks, if I do say it of your blood kin, Tuck. Much good it's ever done you or the twins, either, the old man cutting his daughter off like he did and all. It wasn't none of her fault—I'm not saying it was—but your daddy marrying her and her so young . . . Well, looked like that was the start of his bad luck and it's dogged him ever since."

Ida thumped the biscuit dough as viciously as she had kicked the stove. "I can't help wondering, times, just the same, if *she'd* of had to put up with all I have. Not that I'd name it to your daddy. But a man can stay a fool a long time—and I mean a bigger fool than he's born to be—if he's hooked by a pair of big eyes and a pretty face."

Tuck raised hard eyes but Ida's face was bent over the dough she was kneading, her head full of old grievances. Tuck thought, She's jealous of my mother. Jealous of a drowned woman. He began to feel sick.

"Not as I begrudge her the little she had," Ida said on a virtuous sigh. "She never got much of a chanct, poor little old thing, drownding herself like she did in her own back yard. And for a hatching of biddies."

Tuck lowered his eyes and the paper blurred under them, its blue lines weaving together. He wanted to yell at her to shut up; he didn't need her account of the old tragedy. He didn't have to close his eyes to see the swirling yellow flood waters of the Chattahoochee. He could have told Ida Faraday how it spurted, first through the cracks of the board fence, then pushed the fence down to float before its wild, foaming weight. He remembered how it looked spraying through the cracks and his mother leaping from the porch into the yard to grab at the yeeping balls of fluff scattering from the squawking fool of a hen. It was twelve years ago last spring, but Tuck could still feel the cramp in his fingers on the windowsill and the screams rising to choke him instead of coming out. . . .

"Chickens," Ida said, scornfully. "Looks like your daddy would have wrote them off as a bad job then, don't it? But oh, no. He had to sell his sawmill short and leave out of Laurel Gap to start raising 'em. Been better if he'd stayed up there in the poultry country if you ask me. Couldn't nobody ever tell him a thing, though, onct he set his head. Claimed there was too much competition, wanted to get off to hisself." Her laugh was bitter. "Ask me, I think he just got an itchy foot and had to come down here to South Georgia to scratch it."

Tuck tasted blood where he'd sunk his teeth into his lip. He wished he hadn't fixed her old door if it had to start her on all this. She'd never gone quite this far before in front of him. His stomach was sick and there was a roaring in his ears like the flood waters that had taken his mother. He glued his eyes to his notebook, afraid that if he looked at his stepmother again he would jump up and choke her to silence.

He remembered the first time he'd seen Ida. It must have been soon after they'd moved to Laurel Gap that she came home with his father in the pickup truck. She had climbed down stiffly from the truck with no help from his father, smoothing her flowered dress—pink it was, he recalled, with splashy white flowers on it. Sitting on the door stone, Tuck had watched her coming across the bare-swept yard, poking at her tight-frizzed hair that was so soon to droop into the limp strands of now.

Most clearly of all he remembered her saying, "You're not a-scared of me, are you, sugar? You're Tucker, now ain't you?" And he had scrambled up from the door stone and run to push his face into his Aunt Cleo's apron. He had been four or five then, Tuck reckoned, not old enough to go to school.

Now, Ida said, as if she had caught on that he was sick at his stomach, "I didn't aim to say all that about your mama, Tuck. It was your daddy I had on my mind. Seems like he just got off on the wrong foot somehow and never could take the extry skip to catch up. Like somebody marching outa step. Hard luck's hounded him and he's give in to it. Tom and Clete look like turning out the same way—always changing and looking for some different kind of a job. I don't know what'll happen to them—without they end up in the service." She spread her floured rag and began to roll the biscuit dough on it.

"But you, Tuck. Now, sometimes I get to wondering about you. Maybe it's on account of you being so quiet and all—like you was saving yourself up for . . . I don't know. I just don't know—"

Tuck heard his brothers arguing in the yard. He scraped his books and papers off the table and went to the bedroom, slamming the door so hard the snapshot of Tolly Mayhew fell out of the crack between the mirror and the frame and lay, face down, among the clutter on the dresser. Seeing it there, Tuck began to laugh, painful, heaving laughter that pressed tears out of his eyes and made him clutch at a stitch in his side.

He wanted nothing to do with women. Only hurt came out of it—and it wasn't fair. Not as if he went looking for them; it would be different if that was so. But Elva, then Ida—and now the silly, grinning picture of Tolly Mayhew falling out of the mirror's frame. Let it lie. Tom or Clete could pick it up and stick it back in its place if they wanted to. But a dragging sadness Tuck could not name, much less explain, settled where his rage and pain had burned. It stayed with him until he fell asleep that night.

4

THE WEEK dragged for Tuck. Ida's talk of the past was a heaviness he couldn't shake, expert that he had thought himself at burying troublesome thoughts. And there was another thing. Though he had resolved to put behind him all memory of his encounter with Elva Grimes, he could not avoid seeing her in class.

At first, he refused to even look in her direction, but the refusal itself dug her image into his mind, making his skin burn and the muscle under his eye twitch distractingly. In angry despair he looked boldly at her. She was peeking at him from between her eyelashes, the lids he had longed to touch nearly closed. She quickly lowered her face over her book, but Tuck saw the bright blush flame into it. Was it because he'd caught her looking at him or from shame at what she had done to him?

He told himself it didn't matter. If he told himself enough it would be true, yet the telling kept her on his mind, too. It was like a toothache, nagging and hurting. He thought that if he could talk to Pete Degley—not about Elva, of course; he would never tell anyone about Elva—he would feel better. Then he would be able to bury this new memory as he had the old ones that hurt.

He considered cutting school altogether, but his pride balked at giving Elva the satisfaction of so much power. He would worry through it somehow, he vowed morosely, if it killed him. And it wouldn't; he'd found out long ago that humiliation didn't kill.

The second day of being in the same room with Elva was no better than the first. He found himself looking at her girl friends on the sly, wondering if she'd told them. When he was unable to see any signs that she had, he was briefly comforted, only to fall back again into a dull depression. The third day was the same and the fourth. Tuck thought his luck had run out altogether, for Pete Degley's car was not at the rink those four days when he came from school. He would hang around, watching the work a few minutes, then make his way slowly to the house, dreading to get there.

On Saturday, beside himself with restlessness, he left the dinner table while the others were still eating and wandered down to the rink. He knew the men stopped work at noon on Saturdays, but Pete Degley was getting out of his yellow Chevrolet as Tuck came clear of the peach trees.

"Hi, Faraday. You're just the feller I want to see."

At the blithe greeting the leaden weight of the past days seemed to drop from Tuck.

"Got something I want to show you. Come on inside if you got a few minutes."

Tuck followed Pete into the rink, not sure whether he was glad or sorry to see how nearly completed it looked to be. Several crates were stacked against the wall at the far end of the building. Pete pried a slat from one and drew out a pair of black shoe skates.

"White ones for the ladies, black for the fellows," he said, grinning as he handed the skates to Tuck. "Those look to be somewhere round your size." He watched Tuck handling the skates, careful as if they were made of glass.

Tuck turned them in his hands, liking the smell of new leather and the winking of light on new metal. He spun a wheel with his finger, felt that he should say something, not knowing what. And all the time it was not the skates that pleased him, but Mr. Degley's confidence, the way he had seemed, from the first, to share the great project of the roller rink with Tucker Holland Faraday.

"You being a country boy," Pete said as Tuck handed the skates back to him, "probably never had much truck with roller skates. It's a city sport mostly, of course, but there's got to be a first time for everything. How'd you like to try a pair of these skates out?"

"M-Me, Mr. Degley?" Tuck could feel himself blushing to his collar bones. "I—I c-couldn't—"

"Now hold it, man, hold it." Pete tossed the skates carelessly onto the crate. He strolled over to the bench encircling the beautiful, smooth floor and sat down, motioning Tuck to sit beside him.

"I been getting to know you, Faraday," he said, opening his knife and feeling in his coat pocket for one of the bits of wood he was always picking up after the workmen and stashing away so he'd be sure to have something to whittle on when he wanted it. "All this time we been knocking around here together, watching this place coming up like a big old mushroom out of the ground, I been watching you. Watching and sizing you up, and I've come to the conclusion you just *might* have the makings of a skater. A good skater. Something out of the ordinary. I didn't just jump to that conclusion, either. Like I say, I been getting to know you, you might say studying you considerably. Mighty near since the first time I clapped eyes on you. About a month ago now, little more maybe, since that day you turned up here after the hike you take for your health, school days." His eyes twinkled, but Tuck sensed a seriousness under his little joke.

"Tell you the truth, Faraday, it wouldn't surprise me any if that walk keeps you in good trim. People take to riding more than they do now, they'll be setting the stage for generations without legs."

Expectancy, faintly edged with dread, began to swell within Tuck, increased with Pete Degley's next words.

"What I'm saying, Faraday, is, you've got your body." He stopped as if he wanted to make sure it sank in. Tuck shifted his feet and Pete went on. "This little impediment in your speech don't alter that. Plenty of guys able to spout lectures to great big audiences every night in the week couldn't necessarily play All American football. Or dive sixty feet through a flaming hoop. Or figure-skate to suit *me,* far as that's concerned." He chuckled. "Am I losing you, Faraday?"

"Y-Y-Yes, sir. I mean n-no, sir," Tuck murmured, not knowing what he meant.

"My point is, son—" Pete Degley looked at his knife

as if he had never seen it before, his brows bent, his lip thrust forward. "My point is, you might not could give a lecture, but you might *could* put on any one of the other performances."

The muscle under Tuck's left eye began to twitch, but Pete Degley continued to look at his knife, turning it slowly in his knotty fingers.

"I had me a dream, Tuck, from away back yonder. Had me a lot of them. Most men do, I guess, I don't know."

Tuck stirred uneasily. He didn't like the word dream —though he knew Pete Degley meant daydream.

"You see this big building here. It took a heap of one-week stands in a portable canvas top to get anywheres in sight of it. It took traveling with a second-rate carnival a couple of seasons, with me one half of a second-rate skating team. It took a lot of playing hunches on top of everything else. I believe in mine, seldom had a hunch to let me down." He was suddenly still, his eyes looking beyond Tuck into something dark and secret, the hand with the knife resting on his knee. "Once, I did, though. I followed a hunch and put my trust in a guy and he betrayed it. I had to fire him." He shrugged. "I reckon anybody's liable to make a mistake once—"

Tuck's hands were shaking. He started to shove them into his pockets, remembered Ida's complaining and put them, tightly clenched, on his knee, hoping Mr. Degley wouldn't notice them shaking.

"This rink," Pete said, looking round the enormous building, "isn't but part of the dream I had me so long. It's bigger than this building, my dream is." He began to whittle, thin shavings littering the floor round his feet. "If there's one thing I learned, Faraday, it's to bide my time. But I'm no kid, as you can see—and time can run out. I got a feeling in my old bones it's time to have another go at realizing my dream. You could call it a vision—up here in my hard old head." He sang in a low, husky tone, "It's time, Lord, it's time—"

A shiver slid along Tuck's spine and he was glad of the sunshine lying on the floor under the Miami windows.

"I was a little old shirttail boy when I got a busted knee—I *mean,* boy, really busted, too—on roller skates in Birmingham, Alabama. Hitched onto the tailpiece of a truck and it threw me. My kneecap was splintered up like a china cup. I *mean.*" He shook his head. "I don't recollect how many weeks I was in the hospital, but it must of been a year or more I was hobbling around, left out of it with the other tough kids in the neighborhood. That's what like to killed me, being left out of it. Me, the toughest, braggiest, biggitiest kid in the street!"

Tuck nodded; he knew about being left out, all right.

"I guess I was plenty lucky not being crippled the rest of my life. But it wasn't all luck. I put in some good licks at getting over that knee. Time came when I got those skates out again. My old lady squawled like a scalded cat, but I'd skate anyway—one foot to start with—when she wasn't around. Well, it could of been something else, but for me it was wheels on my feet. And it worked out."

Not meaning to, Tuck exclaimed, "It s-sure did, Mr. Degley. I'll s-say it did!"

He was sorry as soon as it was out, for it looked as if

he had stopped Pete telling him his dream. But his admiration had burst its bonds and he hadn't been able to keep still.

"How would it suit you to slip off down here tonight and try out a pair of these brand-new skates?"

Terror swamped Tuck's glow of admiration. The muscle under his eye started jumping again, so violently that Pete Degley's face dimmed before him. He tried to swallow, but his mouth was dry and his throat ached. His "M-Me, Mr. Degley?" came out in a dry whisper.

"Yeah, you, Tucker Faraday—if I haven't made a mistake and am talking to one of your yellow-haired brothers." Amusement tempered his mild sarcasm. "If the notion don't appeal to you, forget it, son, and no hard feelings. It was just an idea I had." He brushed his pants leg, dropped the sliver of wood that remained from his whittling among the shavings on the floor, and put his knife in his pocket.

"B-B-But—but—"

"You a goat or something, all that butting around?" Pete meticulously adjusted his hat brim, tilting it at a natty angle.

"I—I c-c-couldn't p-pay—" Color washed painfully across his averted face.

Pete turned so sharply Tuck flinched. "I say anything about paying?" He shifted into a drawl. "Could be there'd be money involved, one way or another, but I don't recollect suggesting it—yet. All I wanta know is, would you be interested?"

Tuck's red face twisted with effort. "Y-Yes, sir, I w-would, sir."

Pete Degley stood up and Tuck, numb and tingling as if his legs had gone to sleep, stood, too.

"O.K. You be down here at seven-thirty sharp. And keep it under your hat, hear? There's nothing shady about this, but you can see what it would be if it was to leak out I was giving skating lessons before the joint's open." Tuck could see; he managed a crooked grin. "I was always one," Pete said, "to keep my business close. Especially something you might call experimental."

Going up to the house, Tuck thought, abashed, that he had not given Mr. Degley so much as a thank-you. Thanks for what? He didn't know, yet—but he'd be seeing more of Pete Degley and that was a relief. He had been dreading the completion of the rink as a possible end to the companionship he treasured.

A new gas station had opened in Wesley, and Tom and Clete had got a day's work there. Tuck's father was more disgruntled than usual because he had let the twins take his pickup truck and had no way to get to town for the Saturday shopping.

"If they wasn't so no-account they could of walked," he said, as if he had only now realized the fact. "I was their age, two miles wasn't nothing for me to walk, and it over a mountain, likely as not."

"Guess Tuck's the only walker in this family," Ida said, pursing her lips. "Still and all, My, you wouldn't want to discourage the boys taking advantage of a opportunity that could lead to a part-time job. Why didn't you take them and bring the truck back? Then you'd of had us a way to town."

Tuck paid little attention; such talk was always going

on in the house. For all their grumbling he sometimes thought his family drew a kind of nourishment from it and would have hungered without it.

All afternoon he worked at odd jobs—some that needed doing, some he invented to occupy his time till evening. His father worked beside him at some of the real jobs, taciturn and silent, nursing the grudge against himself for having allowed the twins to take the truck. A pale, mottled cloud obscured the sun along toward feeding time and a fitful wind threatened a cold night.

Whenever Tuck thought about the night goose pimples sprang out on his skin, yet he would not have been without the anticipation, mixed with dread as it was. His brothers drove the rattling old truck into the yard before the early supper Ida slapped petulantly onto the table. She did not sit down with them, snatching her apron off and smoothing the front of her rayon print dress. She had put Myron's plate before him even earlier and carried it to the sink now, her felt bedroom slippers rasping across the worn linoleum.

"You and me," she told Karen with a wink just missing gaiety, "are going to treat ourselves to a hamburger and French fries at the Choice Cafe." She cast an injured look at the twins. "If I got to do my grocery shopping of a night, might as well get *something* out of it, hadn't I?"

"You do that, Ma," Tom said and Clete added with a grin, "You live it up, you and Karen."

From the truck where Myron was waiting a bleat of the horn told his impatience. Ida struggled into her shoes and followed Karen out of the house.

The twins ate voraciously, talking with full mouths of

goings-on in town during the day. Tuck knew they would try to pry the oily dirt from under their fingernails afterwards and set off for the Mayhew place where Tolly could hang on their words, batting her heavily blacked eyelashes and caressing her long pale hair. Tuck finished before them and went to lie on his narrow iron bed. He always found solitude less lonely than being beyond the edge of their empty talk.

He stared at the ceiling he could hardly make out in the evening gloom and listened to the dribble of the shower while they bathed. He pretended to be asleep, his face turned to the wall, when Tom, then Clete, came in to dress for the night's courting. The naked bulb swung slowly after its cord was pulled, making the room appear to rock. The brothers talked as if Tuck were not there. Tom whistled softly between his teeth when he wasn't talking; Clete only talked. Then one of them yanked the cord, the room plunged into darkness, and Tuck heard them go down the hall and out the front door.

He lay a while longer, seeing the rectangle of window gradually shape itself against the dark-blue sky. He did not often have the house to himself. It was like a strange place, the musty room slowly losing the sharp tang of after-shave lotion, the furniture blurred and dark, the window growing lighter as darkness claimed the room. The branches of a shrub scraped the pane. Pete Degley's voice echoed in Tuck's mind: "I had me a dream . . ."

The dripping of a tap sounded loud enough to have been inside his ear, and Tuck rose and groped his way to the bathroom. Putting the light on, he blinked at the disorder his brothers had left behind them. Sodden towels, the rusty spigot of the homemade shower not properly turned off which accounted for the drip-drip of water into the tub, a twisted tube with a plump worm of shaving cream drooping from its mouth, soiled shirts hanging from the peg on the door. It was a familiar sight—one he had heard his stepmother grumble about countless times and scarcely noticed. Tonight, it vaguely offended him.

Quickly, he tidied the room and showered in lukewarm water that began to run cold before he was done. He plastered his wet hair down with the comb, scowled at a tender pink spot on his chin that would be a pimple by morning. What the heck? He'd been luckier than Tom and Clete with his complexion. Not that he gave a hoot, he reminded himself. He didn't have to worry about what Tolly Mayhew thought of him. An unbidden thought of Elva Grimes's eyelids flickered across his mind and he stared it down in the tiny mirror over the washbowl.

He took his old plaid jacket from the hall tree, shrugging into it as he went out, closing the front door as softly as if the house were full of sleeping family. As he entered the orchard the excitement of the morning came back to him, making his heart thud, setting the muscle under his eye to jumping. Maybe he was as big a fool as most people thought he was, sticking his neck out for goodness knew what. Then guilt struck at him sharply. Pete Degley was his friend. Whatever his doubts, that wasn't one. Pete Degley was his friend.

5

THE WIRING of the rink had not been completed and the rays of a gasoline lantern sent inadequate light about the enormous building. Tuck stood just inside and stared with unbelieving eyes at Pete Degley. The familiar, wiry form of the man was transformed into a vision of grace Tuck could not have imagined. In long swinging strides it crossed the floor, described graceful arcs, whirled like a dervish till it was two, three, half a dozen figures spinning gradually to one as it slowed and stopped.

"Hi, Faraday. Come on and let's get started." He was scarcely short of breath, while Tuck felt that his was rationed. Surely Mr. Degley did not think that *he* could learn to do that! It gave him the shakes to think of such a thing.

Even so, Tuck could not believe the clumsiness of his body when he had the skates on his feet. His trembling shamed him. To hide his fear of falling he scorned the railing—only to crash to the floor. He seemed to have grown an extra pair of legs, and even when he managed not to fall his feet refused to do his bidding.

Pete Degley was unperturbed.

"You'll get the hang of it. Just loosen up. Watch." And he would glide away, holding himself like a slow-motion film while Tuck looked on, covered with self-consciousness and embarrassment. He had Tuck go through certain postures again and again while holding the despised rail.

"You take these dancers, Faraday. You'd swear they had wings, the things they do on the stage with a thousand eyes on 'em. You wouldn't believe all the hours they sweat out, holding to that barre while they whip their muscles into shape. It's not wings—or wheels—that does the trick, man. It's work. Work and sweat."

But Tuck didn't get the hang of it. The ease of Pete Degley's motions made it look as if there was nothing to it, but when Tuck tried to follow his patient instructions he tensed up all over—like his throat before he attempted a long sentence—and the results had all the grace of a cow in a parlor.

His failure filled him with an impotent rage. Little kids could do what he couldn't; he'd seen them once or twice, rolling along with crazy speed. Maybe that was it, he thought. What Pete Degley had mastered at nine or ten couldn't be begun at nearly sixteen with any hope of success. His anger spread to include Mr. Degley, the one person in all the world Tuck hadn't suspected of adding to his long humiliation. His tension mounted with his anger, while at the same time he was determined to justify Pete's confidence, no matter how crazy it was.

Stubbornly Tuck struggled, making a show of himself with flailing arms and bitten lip. When the lesson ended he waited with bowed head for Mr. Degley to tell him to forget it, that his hunch had let him down once more. But Pete was as cheery as a redbird in spring as he told Tuck to come back the next night.

"Don't worry, Faraday. You'll do fine—soon as you quit trying too hard. So you spill, so what? Ever see a little shaver learning to walk? Notice how he'll go down and get up and pitch off again?" He gave Tuck an unruffled good night, took his lantern and went away to his private world at the Dixie Belle Motel a mile up the highway.

In the morning Tuck's stiff muscles protested at so much as mixing a batch of chicken mash. And he couldn't see that the next night was much better, though he spent more time on his feet than on the floor. One thing stood out, raw and bitter, in his mind: he was his father's son and doomed to failure, no matter what he undertook.

Tuck could not always get away from the house without its being known, and once Ida said curiously, seeing him take his jacket from the peg, "Where you going to, this time of night, Tuck?"

"Out," Tuck said, not looking at her.

"That's no way to speak to your ma," Myron said, but he sounded dutiful rather than angry.

"He might could be getting that age," Cletus observed, looking owlishly at Tom who grinned.

"You hush up, Clete," Ida shrilled. "I'll not have that kinda talk in my house." Tuck smiled, zipping his jacket. He knew his stepmother's sporadic bursts of primness.

"I l-like the n-night air," he said and went out, hoping they'd think he'd gone for a walk. They could think what they pleased, he told himself, glancing over his shoulder at the lighted windows of the house. He couldn't remember anything he had ever done that had been of any real interest to them. Why should they bother now?

On Tuesday, the fourth night, the miracle occurred.

Arriving, Tuck saw the rink ablaze with light and his heart sank. His awkwardness would surely be all the more apparent in such a glare.

"Brought us a little music along," Pete said after Tuck had his skates on. His cheerfulness made Tuck feel sour as a half-ripe persimmon. He watched Pete fiddle with the portable player, plugging it into an outlet, setting the record carefully on the turntable, opening the volume control. The "Skaters' Waltz" blared forth and Tuck broke into a cold sweat. Pete turned the volume down slightly and, not giving Tuck so much as a glance, began to circle about the rink, his arms folded across his chest. Tuck moved forward cautiously, the baby learning to walk, not much more confident than on the night he began.

It was moments before he realized that something was happening inside his head. It was filling with sound, with the music Pete Degley had brought. It pulsed through him, supporting, urging him on to a daring beyond anything he had dreamed. It took possession of his legs, his feet, his entire being. Awkwardness dropped away, he forgot the floor beneath him, felt his spirit break free of the heaviness of his body and spread still-damp wings in flight. He had no thought of where he was nor of Pete Degley. All his awareness was caught and held by the sound in his ears and the motion, so strangely effortless, on which he floated like a leaf on a stream. When, at last, Pete shut the player off, Tuck brought himself to a smooth, unwavering stop.

"See?" Pete said, quietly. "Just like I said, you've got the hang of it." As if it were not a miracle, as if he had known all the time it would be like this. Trembling with exaltation, Tuck put his skates away. I did it, he was thinking in time to the music still throbbing against his temples. I did it.

"Big player will be hooked up by tomorrow night," Pete said on a wide yawn. "Jeez, I could do with some shut-eye. How about you?" And Tuck, who felt that he need never sleep again, nodded while happiness swept over him in waves that made him dizzy. "We're gonna have us a number for opening night that'll make some of these crackers sit up and take notice," Pete chuckled. "Night, Faraday. See you tomorrow."

When Tuck arrived, five nights later, the girl was sitting on the bench drinking a Coke. Seeing her, Tuck felt so sharply the pain of Elva Grimes's ring against his ear that he put his hand to it before he knew what he was doing.

"Hi, Faraday," Pete called. "Want you to meet my wife. Lily, this is my friend, Tuck Faraday, the guy I been telling you about."

Friend, Tuck thought, the taste of bile bitter in his mouth. Big deal. Meet my wife. He couldn't have heard it right. Mr. Degley didn't have a wife! He was Pete Degley, Tuck Faraday's friend. . . . This girl sitting on the bench as if she owned it didn't look like anybody's wife. If he'd said his daughter—but he hadn't said that, he'd said wife. Where had she been? Hidden at the Dixie Belle Motel? Why hadn't Pete ever mentioned her? Tuck felt hollow inside, bereft and betrayed. Pete Degley had been his only friend. . . .

The girl Lily took a long pull at the straw, mashed it into the Coke bottle, and smiled at Tuck. She was small, with a wide mouth and brown skin, the hair lying about her little neck as smooth and straight as pine needles. Tuck's look, moving sullenly from the tilt of her brows, across her breasts lifting the lemon-colored sweater, down the line of her shabby tights, came to rest on her soiled white skates. The leather looked soft as old gloves, and worn.

"All right." Pete's voice was like a slap. "Let's get this show on the road. Get your gear on, Faraday. Lily, you wanta warm up some?"

In the center of the rink Lily looked smaller than ever —like a child showing off. But she wasn't a child. She was Mrs. Degley. Tuck watched her, his hands clumsily lacing his skates. Lily, poised on toes, made a showy turn and darted away with the swiftness of light. She dipped, turned, pirouetted, as unaware of it all as a butterfly hovering over a flower.

Why had Pete done this? The question seared Tuck's mind. That dream of his he'd starting telling and never finished, the number for opening night that was to make folks sit up and take notice—bits and pieces of Pete Degley's talk over the weeks tumbled after the burning *why* without answering it. He could have prepared Tuck—

"Faraday," Pete shouted. "Get the lead outa your feet, man. You want Lily to steal the show?"

Steal the show! She was the show—Lily Degley. Mrs. Pete Degley. It was a trap, of course, rigged to make a fool of Tuck the dummy. Rage, hot and terrible, boiled up in Tuck. Against Pete Degley. Against Lily. Against Elva Grimes and Link Grover and, most of all, against himself. This time he wasn't taking it lying down. This time he'd show them—Pete and this Lily, Mr. and Mrs. Degley. He hadn't sweated his bones out for them to make a fool of him.

He knotted the laces of his skates with a savage tug and was under the railing. Forcing himself to skate slowly, he kept his eyes on Lily, still showing off out there in the center, cutting figures so intricate his eyes could barely follow them. He skated round her a couple of times, picking up speed very gradually, drawing in a bit, shortening the distance between them. Each time he was almost within reach of her she eluded him and he could see the smile on her face, mocking him. He darted sidewise, turned, stopped short in front of her. But with never a flaw in grace or swiftness, she escaped him.

Tuck had no clear plan of what he would do when he reached her—only his determination to show them. It absorbed his fear and, as he pressed on, even his anger so that he felt only powerful and predatory, intent upon the chase. He had no sense of the passing of time, but he saw that Lily was tiring, her breath coming through parted lips, her forehead glazed with sweat, the brown hair whipping out from her shoulders when she pivoted.

The moment bore down upon him. NOW. He had only to put out his hands and seize her—but she flung her arms up, fingers meeting above her head. Dizzily she spun before his burning eyes to stop, panting, hands held toward him, her glistening face a wide, disarming smile. Bewildered, he took her hands. Music poured from somewhere, from everywhere, and Tuck and Lily skated together toward the blur of Pete Degley's face.

"Not bad," Pete said, softly. "Not bad if I do say so myself."

Tuck didn't know where or how his fury had gone—only that he had lost it, skating with Lily. Her name no longer pierced his mind like a barb. She was Mr. Degley's wife, whatever her age, wherever she had been. The *why* of Mr. Degley's secrecy had died like a guttered candle and he knew Pete Degley's dream—all of it: a roller rink with a pair of skaters to draw the crowds. It would be a thing of Pete Degley's making, his creation. But why him? Why Tucker Holland Faraday? Pete could have partnered Lily and saved himself the grind of teaching Tuck. . . .

Sitting on the bench to get his wind, Tuck felt a tap on his shoulder and jerked his head round to see Pete standing over him.

"See what I mean, Faraday? Not just any Tom, Dick, or Harry could do this job. Not like I want it done."

Tuck wiped his face with his sleeve. "Y-Yes, sir."

"Now you get your second wind," Pete Degley went on, walking back and forth in front of Tuck, "and we'll run through a few of the things I got in mind." He put on his skates and circled the rink a time or two to warm up. While Tuck's breath was still coming hard Pete said, "Ready, Lily? We'll just give him an idea," and Lily was beside him, their crossed hands joined.

Tuck's eyes ached with the intensity of his watching. Consternation gnawed at him. What if he couldn't do it? And to have to get out there and try with *her* looking on . . . He leaned on the rail, trying to absorb every move. If his eyes and his brain could take it in, he would force his body to perform.

When his turn came his heart pounded and his mouth was like sawdust. Pete's easy voice sounded far away, directing him. He was jumpy for fear Lily would put her two cents worth in, woman-like, but she didn't; she, too, might have been a beginner, her eyes and ears for Pete alone. Tuck could see—and was impressed by—her deep respect for Pete Degley. He decided she was no teen-ager in spite of her looks and, grudgingly, he allowed her to rise a notch or two in his esteem.

It was all changed now, anyway, Tuck thought, when Pete told them they'd had enough and he took his skates off. Something had been torn, split apart—something dear to him.

"You're going to be O.K., Faraday," Pete said. "You're shaping up pretty much like I had you figured to." He put a hand on Lily's arm, his fingers squeezing gently. "You and Lily are going to bring this act off. You'll be a good team, easy on the eyes, too. Young folks want to see other young folks doing things they can envy. Even if my knee would hold up, I wouldn't undertake to partner Lily in this. Didn't plan it that way."

"Better put your jacket on before you go out," Lily said, smiling at Tuck a little shyly.

Under the cold, bright stars, going home, Tuck thought of the two riding up the highway in the yellow Chevrolet, stopping at the Dixie Belle. His face burned. Mr. and Mrs. Degley. He'd have to get used to that. . . .

Suddenly a faint tingle of elation quivered through his bewilderment and weariness. Maybe—in time—he could even feel that something had been added to, not split off from, his friendship with Pete Degley. Whatever happened, he had come a long way since September.

6

PETE DEGLEY brought the sweating bottles of Coke from the cooler, handed Lily's straw to her with a wink, and sat with them while they cooled off. October had gone and the countryside was brown with November. The rink was cold when Tuck came down to practice now at night. Pete skated, too, to keep his circulation going. But his brown eyes were as hot and sharp as ever, missing no false move, and he was as quick to bawl at Lily as at Tuck.

"Take that drink easy, boy," he cautioned Tuck now. "A cold swig can give a guy mighty sharp stummick cramps and him sweated up like you are." He didn't have to remind Lily of such things. She sipped daintily, bright, curious eyes on Tuck.

"Won't your folks be surprised, Tucker, when they see you out there, opening night? I don't see how you kept it from them what you're doing, your house as close as it is."

Tuck covered his pleasure with a shrug. "They d-don't

b-bother about me." He had long been able to bring out a few words without halting when he talked to Pete, but Lily's presence still clamped his throat a little.

"What'll they say when they do find out?" Lily persisted. "What will they think?"

Tuck braced himself, pulling a tough look over the hurt that was always ready to flare up.

"They think I'm l-looney."

Lily said something under her breath, then blurted, "Families. I'm glad Pete's all the family I've got." And not for the first time Tuck experienced a vague, faint pain at the intimate look that passed between Pete and Lily Degley.

"You should of seen her the first time she showed up at my rink, Tucker," Pete chuckled. "That old mobile one I was operating then. Fierce as a little old banty rooster. Wasn't about to take a thing off of anybody. Specially me! I liked her spunk, me that had made up my mind way back about women. And when I saw what she could do with a pair of skates—" He whistled, long and low. "Little old State Kid, full of fight for the whole blame world and no wonder, pushed around like she'd been from one foster family to another—all of 'em looking for her to come a cropper. Right, Lil?" He drew himself up, the little fires flaming bright behind his eyes. "I gave Lily a name she didn't have to be ashamed of and protection she'd of died before letting on she needed. And I don't mind telling you, Tuck, she's given me a wife I been proud of from the minute I put that ring on her finger. Not to mention getting me a skating artiste to boot."

Tuck slowly digested Lily's life story, so briefly given

by Pete Degley. He was violently startled by Pete's next words, added like a postscript. "Only trouble Lily and me ever come anywheres close to having was none of her making. If I'd read her signals right that guy I fired wouldn't ever have been connected with our business. That was my fumble—and, like I say, I reckon a man's entitled to one, provided he don't make it twice."

Pete's intense brown eyes stared straight into Tuck's worried gray ones and Tuck was satisfied. Not that he had really believed Mr. Degley was warning him. But he felt better all the same after the long honest look.

"My mother—my r-real mother—died when I wasn't b-but three years old," Tuck heard himself saying, breaking the silence that had held them a moment. He was astonished when it came out. He hadn't meant to say it, but now he had he said more, not trying to stop it, giving in to a need he had never recognized as such. "She d-d-drowned in a f-flood and nobody but me s-saw it happen."

He looked at their faces—Lily's paling with shock, Pete's drawing in tight, his crooked mouth thin with a look like anger. Lily's hand came forward, impulsively, to touch his arm. To his horror he felt tears sting his eyeballs and looked down to hide them.

"I never told anybody b-before," he said, his voice coming rough to keep from breaking. "They—my folks—think I was t-too little to remember. But I remember it p-plain as day. My—My dad got to the house before the w-w-water was over my head. I recollect him p-picking me up and neighbors b-bringing a boat and t-taking us out of there—"

"Oh, Tucker." Lily's little moan was balm on a wound too old to be more than a scar. She said, "Anyhow she must've loved you—while you had her. My mother gave me away. Before I was born." Her face was small with grief.

"Lily," Pete said, anger still round his lips but his voice softer than Tuck had ever heard it. He had never heard any man's voice so soft. "Lily girl. You know we put that behind us where it belongs to be."

As Lily flipped her hair over her shoulders and smiled at Pete, Tuck thought, dazed by the discovery, Mine's behind me, too—where it belongs to be.

Pete said in the same soft voice, "Crummy things happen to kids, things that hadn't ought to happen to them. But you're not kids now, you two. You're people." He snapped his fingers, suddenly all business. "O.K. Do me your big turn once more. Remember, Faraday, to spin her the full count of sixteen bars. And you want to smooth out your revolutions, Lily. They've got to improve considerable before they come anywheres near suiting me."

Back at work, Tuck felt strangely light. He was glad he had told. He was glad Pete Degley hadn't given him a word of sympathy, showing only his anger that crummy things could happen to kids. And Tuck was glad he had not left out the part about his father saving his life. He gave himself over to the music, which was quite different from what Pete had started with and took some getting used to. But Tuck preferred it now and often went through the orchard humming bits of "Swan Lake" or "Waltz of the Flowers." Pete's explanation of the change had taken hold of Tuck's mind, given him an excited lift.

" 'Skaters' Waltz' and 'Glowworm' are O.K. for the crowd to skate to. Artistes need something better. You can't do a big act without you hear and think and skate big. Tchaikovsky and Ravel are the ones for that."

Before mid-December the skating rink was done. Tuck could not look around the vast interior, smelling of new lumber and cement, without a glow of personal pride. He felt a part of it. Not only because he had learned to skate in it and was to have a part in helping Pete Degley realize the dream. The building had somehow got under Tuck's skin and into his blood with the first blocks laid and the first nails driven.

Soon Wesley and the highway flaunted posters heralding the opening of Pete Degley's ELYSIUM ON WHEELS. Tuck turned the words in his mind, delighted with Pete's cleverness. Lily told him that Fidelia, Cantrell, Enfield, and Magnolia had posters, too. Tuck thought of her riding round the country, watching the advertisements go up. He had often wondered what she did with her spare time. No house to keep, no children to look after—he had never imagined a married woman like Lily. But then he had never imagined anyone like Lily. Or Pete. When he thought of one now, he thought of the other. Already the days when he had known Pete Degley as a loner seemed far away.

Nightly rehearsals continued, with Pete driving Tuck relentlessly. He managed to work in an extra two hours on Sunday mornings and pointed out that the Christmas vacation would afford them two weeks of afternoons. He brushed aside Tuck's uneasy feelings that it was on account of him that money was being lost due to the delayed opening.

"I don't know of any law that says this rink's got to open before I'm good and ready for it to," he said, grinning at Tuck's long face. "Better we let holidays and what goes with 'em wind up, anyhow. Folks will want somewheres to go and something to do after. And you get the benefit of the practice. I've put you through faster than I could most as it is."

Sunday mornings were easy for Tuck. He had only to wait till Myron, Ida, and Karen left the house for Pine Hill Baptist Church when he could go down to the rink without excuse or explanation, or watching to see if curious eyes observed him. He always felt safe when he reached the orchard; so far as he knew no one ever used the path but himself, the others taking the red-rutted little road that led from the highway to the yard. But on Sundays he didn't have to worry about being seen. Tom and Clete always turned in again after chores and breakfast to catch up the rest they'd missed the night before, hanging around in town or dancing out at Danny's Den, this side of the Dixie Belle Motel.

"Wouldn't hurt you boys any to go to preaching onct in a while," Ida might remark piously, rushing to get herself ready. Myron, looking unnatural in his good brown suit, sided with neither his wife nor his sons. "You used to go, Tuck, when you was a little feller." His stepmother's look left Tuck unmoved.

When there was talk of the opening at home, Tuck was mute as a stone. He took special care to perform his duties about the place to meet his father's satisfaction, hoping to avoid being a target for attention. Since the appearance of the posters there was considerable talk at school. Tuck heard Cletus tell Jenny Morrow the rink was as good as on his dad's land and Jenny, not to be outdone, came back with a smug, "I've got a date to go to the opening with Link. Whenever it is."

It gave Tuck a jolt to think of Link Grover being there when he and Lily did their number. Even now, with the days going too fast, bringing closer too quickly the unveiling of his secret, it was hard for Tuck to think of the little world of the rink including outsiders. He was reluctant to risk its warmth and safety by admitting his former world—that world in which he had walked alone and alien.

In Wesley interest in roller skating broke out like an epidemic. Grade school kids with shiny new Sears Roebuck skates plied to and fro on the choicest paved areas in town along with those who managed on old rusty skates, oiled and adjusted to feet they hadn't been bought for. The long paved walk from the street to the entrance of the courthouse was full of them; so was the smooth, newer sidewalk in front of the Methodist Church.

"It won't hurt business a bit," Pete Degley said. "Let 'em practice up. Hasn't got out how you spend *your* spare time, has it?"

Tuck said he didn't think so. He hoped Tom and Clete hadn't nosed it out and kept still so as to spring it when it would please them most. Cletus was a master hand at that sort of thing.

Then, one afternoon at the beginning of the Christmas vacation, Karen followed Tuck to the orchard. He turned at the edge of bare peach trees, hearing the frail snap of a twig, and saw her a few yards behind him, her eyes round and her hand over her mouth.

"Go on back to the house," he said, quietly but with a new authority in his tone that was not lost on Karen, though the absence of his stammer was.

"You ain't the boss of me," Karen retorted, but uneasily.

Tuck advanced a step toward her and Karen backed off, her face turning red.

"You heard me." He gave her the old grim stare.

Karen took another step backward, her lip thrust out and quivering. "I can go anywhere you can," she flared. Tuck kept his eyes on her. "Aw, you're mean to me, Tuck," she whined. "I hate you! I hate you wors'n I do Tom and Clete. You're just a big dum—"

"Don't you say it."

Karen's eyes filled with tears and, to his astonishment, Tuck felt himself softening. What was she, after all, but a lonesome little kid with nobody to play with? He knew about lonesomeness. Confused, he stammered, "I—I got b-business of my own to t-tend to. I can't fool with you t-tagging after me."

"What bizness?" She wiped her nose with the back of a chubby hand.

"I'll t-tell you sometime, maybe. If you do like I say." Undecided, Karen shifted her feet while a calculating look slid into her pale eyes. "Go on, now. Get b-back to the house."

Without another word, Karen turned and plodded

toward the house. When she was out of sight Tuck went on down to the rink. It would be a joke on him, he thought, if his kid sister was the one to smell out the secret.

He saw Pete's yellow Chevrolet parked alongside the building and forgot Karen. Lily was lacing her skates. She said, "Hi, Tuck," scarcely looking up. "Pete had to go to Fidelia with a man on business. He said for us to go ahead without him."

Blood washed against Tuck's temples. He stood still, looking down at Lily as she tied and knotted the laces.

"Seems like it would break my heart if we let Pete down with this act, Tucker," she said. "He's counting on it so—on us."

Tuck nodded. "It's his d-dream."

"He told you about that?" She studied her hands. They were almost as brown as Pete's, though it was winter and the sun pale and distant most days. "He surely does think a lot of you." She looked up, her eyes warm with her smile. "Well, let's get at it then, Tuck."

It was strange, at first, not having Pete there. Tuck was fumble-fingered putting his skates on, starting the music. He glided round the edge of the rink a few times, keeping his distance from Lily. But when they began to work he had thought only for improving his skating. He knew he would never be satisfied now till he was as good a skater as Lily. Or better.

They went through the number again and again, and Lily could have been a stick of kindling wood instead of a woman when he held her hands or grasped her small, thin waist to lift her. He didn't even know when Pete Degley came into the building and stood, leaning against the wall, his hat on the back of his head, his eyes following them.

"Not bad," Pete said at the end. "Not bad if I do say so myself." It was, Tuck knew by now, as high a form of praise as Pete would grant them at rehearsals.

"Hitched me a ride back," Pete explained. "That town's as full of our ads as it can stick. Bet we'll have might' near as many from there as from Wesley." He moved as if he were strung on wires and every one charged with electricity. "Looks like the fifteenth is going to be O.K. for opening, kids. I set that date in my head a ways back when I saw how Tucker was shaping up." He winked at Tuck. "Don't believe I'm going to have to change it."

The fifteenth of January was less than a month away. A coldness struck at Tuck under his sweaty clothing. It struck at him again as he went through the orchard. The sun, fragment of a red-gold sphere too huge to look real, hung in pink and violet clouds, the bare branches of the Faradays' pecan trees limbed stark against it. Tuck liked sunsets, but he preferred summer ones. This one looked bruised by the cold, the farm buildings brown and bleak. It would be the kind of night on which he woke for no reason and, snug under his quilts, felt pity for the chickens and other creatures at its mercy.

The supper fire crackled in Ida's despised wood stove. Tuck spread his hands above it.

"You fixed that door pretty good, I reckon," Ida said, as if saying so pained her. "Cooks better, looks like."

The sounds of a TV Western galloped from the front room and ricocheted from the walls. Tuck went up the hall and looked in at the front room door. Karen lay on her stomach before the television set, run-over high-heeled shoes dangling from her waving feet. The picture went off for a commercial and Karen turned glazed eyes to Tuck.

"I know where you went to, this afternoon," she said and struggled into a sitting position.

Anxiety stirred in Tuck. He started to turn away but didn't. It wouldn't hurt to find out how much she knew. Karen was not reluctant to tell him, though he could detect signs of wariness under the smirk on her face.

"You went in that big new building, that skating rink!"

Tuck tried hard to appear indifferent. "So what. I like to t-talk to M-Mr. Degley."

"Ha. They's signs down there that say No Trespassing." Karen kicked one of the shoes off and wriggled her toes. "I guess I can read."

Tuck wagged his head solemnly. "Yeah. It's a good thing, t-too. Those signs aren't just a'woofin'. Haven't s-seen anybody m-messing around there, have you?"

Karen considered, looked at him sharply. "Then how come you can go down there and go inside and it not open yet, Mr. Biggity?"

"I'm Mr. D-Degley's friend. I told you—I like to t-talk to him."

"You wasn't talking when I saw you. Mr. Degley wasn't even there, neither! It was a girl—and you and her were skating—"

"Wh-What're you t-talking about?" Tuck's mouth was dry as a bone.

"You and that girl," Karen snapped, trying to cover

her uneasiness with back talk. She tossed her head, the taffy-colored hair slipping on her shoulders.

"Y-You didn't c-come back to the house," Tuck accused, struggling to get the words out in his agitation.

"So what," Karen muttered, unable to hide her fear, not looking at Tuck. "I'm not a-scared of any old signs. Ha!" But her voice quivered.

Tuck stepped into the room. Standing over Karen, he could see her hands begin to shake. "You t-tell me what you know," he said, measuring the words, pain gripping his face muscles.

"I'm not obliged to," Karen said, looking nervously toward the door, signs of screeching for her mother gathering in her face.

Tuck's hands itched to grab her shoulders and shake her till her teeth rattled. To control them he pressed them tightly against his sides. This would take careful handling or Pete's surprise would be spoiled before Tuck so much as saw him again—if it hadn't been already. He swallowed painfully, willing his voice to quietness.

"Y-You are obliged to, Karen." He knelt beside her, leaned forward a little so that his face was close to hers. She drew back, beginning to fiddle with the ends of her hair. "You b-broke the law. If you don't t-talk to me you can talk to the sh-sheriff."

The blatant voice of the commercial rattled in the silence between them, then Karen whimpered, "I ain't a-scared of no old shuriff—"

Tuck swung from threats to bribery, hating the silkiness of his voice when he heard it. "You w-want a s-secret—just between us t-two?"

She nodded.

"Have you told anybody you s-saw me?"

She shook her head.

"You s-swear?"

She pulled a face as pious as Ida's going-to-church one. "It's wrong to swear."

Tuck made a derisive sound. "I d-don't mean cuss, knot-head. I mean v-vow."

"Cross my heart and hope to die." Karen made the sign, staring at him, interest getting the better of her fear. "There wasn't nobody to tell," she added. "Mama was over at Mayhews'. I just came in here and started to watching TV." In a burst of frankness she added, "I was scared to tell. Kind of—"

Tuck sat, hunching still closer to her. "Well, you're r-right. I *was* s-skating. With Mrs. D-Degley." He swallowed, the sound popping drily against his ears. "We— We're going to do a number for the opening n-night. To s-surprise everybody. Mr. Degley, h-he's been teaching me. He didn't w-want anybody to know t-till the big opening night." He had to swallow again. Karen's eyes were like saucers; she breathed snuffily, caught in the exhilaration of sharing the secret. Hope stole through Tuck's consternation.

"I won't l-let on if you don't. I won't t-tell Mr. Degley you s-snuck down there past those signs he put up and s-spied on his act. I won't even be m-mad at you—if you keep our s-secret. M-Mine and yours. C-Course—" He looked away from her, bringing a deep sigh up to hiss slowly through his teeth. "Course I don't know if you're g-grown-up enough . . . m-most kids would blab."

"I'm grown-up enough, Tuck," Karen cried, popping

her hand over her mouth as Tuck frowned and looked quickly over his shoulder at the open door. "I'm grown-up enough," she whispered, her eyes shining and her round face pink. "Honest I am. Cross my—"

"O.K. then," Tuck interrupted, whispering too. He fumbled in his pocket, brought out a bright blue ball of bubble gum, yielded he couldn't remember when by a vending machine. He wiped the lint from it with tenderness, grateful to it. He soberly proffered it. "T-To complete the deal," he said.

The sudden tears in Karen's avid eyes gave him a curious wrench under his breastbone. Why, she was lonesomer than he had ever guessed, ever bothered to notice, he thought, sitting with her for a moment while she sucked at the candy coating of the gum. He felt limp inside, wrung out from the past moments—yet somehow solaced, too, as if he had put out a hand in need and touched one in greater need. He guessed he had never done that before, come to think of it. He'd done it only to save his own skin, but he was glad he hadn't scared her to secrecy. He felt quite sure she wouldn't tell.

Slowly, he got to his feet and Karen, with a last bright look, turned onto her stomach again and faced her cowboy, crouched amid boulders on the TV screen. Tuck crossed the hall and entered the bedroom.

Cletus was sitting on his bed, looking at the Sears catalog in the waning light. A glance showed Tuck the guitars pictured on the thin page and Clete's pencil check beside one.

"I aim to start savin' up, first of the year, I vow, and

send off for this thing," Clete declared. "Man, I mean. That's a pretty git-tar." The rare sociability slipped past Tuck. He hurriedly changed his shirt and pants. "Feller down in Wesley gives lessons and I got a feeling I could pick it up easy." Clete began to tap his foot and moan the line of a folk song, his head moving with the rhythm, the lank sweep of his garish hair swaying. Suddenly he shut the catalog and threw it from him, his singing silenced as though by the closing of the book.

Hurrying out, Tuck guessed Tom's progress with Tolly Mayhew had exceeded Clete's and Clete had been salving his wounded pride with pictures in the old wish book. So what was it to him, Tuck thought irritably. Clete could take care of himself, all right. Going soft over Karen was enough for one day; he wasn't going to take on his brother's disappointment in love. But the laugh, prompted by the thought of Cletus mooning over the guitars in the catalog, somehow fizzled out before it got past Tuck's throat.

7

ON THE Saturday before Christmas the Faradays piled into the truck and went to town.

"You care about going, Tuck?" Ida said, reaching her black plastic purse from the shelf above the sink. "You still got your work clothes on."

Tuck shook his head. Pete had scheduled an extra hour of practice for the morning and Tuck was relieved that the family would be out of the way. The gas station part-time job had not materialized for the twins, but one of them was called on now and then and today both were employed. Ida and Karen had Christmas shopping and Myron, over-whelmed by his womenfolk, would hang around town waiting for them.

"You see to my biddies then," Ida reminded Tuck, glancing into the cracked mirror on the kitchen wall and poking at the tag of hair that was always sliding free of its moorings. She had a clutch of chicks Myron had let her take over for such egg money as might result in future.

There had been bad luck with some of the chickens during the recent cold spell. They had got the "pip" and several had died in spite of Tuck's doctoring. The sickness hadn't spread to the point of disaster, however, and now the weather had turned spring-mild as it often did in Georgia winters. Clouds like baby blankets hung in a pale blue sky and the sun smiled benignly on the brown landscape.

"No telling when we'll be back," Tuck's father said dourly, his look on Karen in her red coat. Her stout legs emerged from its hem, naked to the cuffs of her bobby socks. She had talked fishnet stockings for weeks; Tuck, half ashamed of his softness, hoped his stepmother would buy her some in Wesley today. "You let wimmen folks loose in stores and you have had it," Myron grumbled. Tuck grinned at his father and received an unexpected flicker of response.

When they had gone Tuck stood in the open doorway, breathing the balmy air. He could hear the hens' clucks and ark-ark-arks drifting down from the long house and wire runs. The calf bawled and was answered with the cow's rumble. The pecan trees threw fragile shadows on the leaf-strewn ground beneath them. Sunlight bathed the broken-down tractor at the edge of the grove and sparrows twittered on the barn roof.

A sense of well-being, gentle as the air, flowed into Tuck. His aloneness, so different from the shut-in aloneness when the family were about, was peace, pure as the sparkling water from remembered mountain springs. Below the orchard the rink waited. In a little while Pete and Lily would be there and he would join them and his world would be complete.

He thought he would redd up the house a little, since Ida hadn't had time to do it. He was about to close the door when Tolly Mayhew came round the corner of the house. She'd been running, her face flushed and her coat hanging open.

"They gone a'ready?" she panted.

Tuck nodded, letting his hand fall from the door while his peace shattered as if a blast of dynamite had gone off in the sunny dooryard. Tolly kicked the ground, sand spraying round her shoe.

"Oh, shoot! I was aiming to catch a ride with them. Tom said they were working today. All of them go?" She looked past Tuck into the untidy kitchen.

"Yep. They all went."

"All but you." Tolly's black-fringed eyes measured him. "Poor old Tuck. You hadn't ought to let them leave you to bear the brunt of everything all the time like they do."

"Thanks for nothing," Tuck said, smart-alecky and rude and ashamed of it almost immediately. But Tolly didn't seem to notice. She was looking at him curiously.

"Don't you stutter any more?"

"C-Could be." He wished she'd take herself off. He was due at the rink at ten and it was nine or after now. He said, "Too bad you m-missed your ride."

Tolly shrugged. "Oh, I'll get me a ride, don't worry. Daddy might could take me—but I wanted to go real early and get my shopping done. What I've got left to do, I mean." It didn't look to Tuck as if she were in any hurry to get anything done, hanging around and waiting to see whether he had quit stammering. She was a long-legged blonde, not bad-looking if she'd leave half that black junk off her eyes. He had never really looked at her before, though she had been around since the Faradays moved down here from North Georgia. Tuck resented whatever it was that made him look at her now; he hadn't time—and he didn't like not being the boss of his eyes.

He drew back a little into the kitchen and put his hand on the door again. Tolly took the hint. She turned and walked slowly away with a disappointed look to her back. Suddenly she half turned her head, calling over her shoulder, "You better watch out, Tuck, or you're liable to turn out the best-looking one of the Faraday boys. But don't you tell Tom I said so, hear?" Her laugh rose, high and thin, on the springlike air.

Tuck pushed the door to. He looked at the clock's face, blurred from the spatterings of Ida's endless frying. Ten past nine. He began to wash the egg-encrusted plates, ignoring the fact that his hands shook a little. He rinsed the coffee cups and thumped them onto the drainboard. He didn't bother sweeping the floor. *Poor old Tuck.* Why couldn't any of the girls he knew be like Lily Degley? But of course he knew why; no one was like Lily.

His bed and his brothers' were a tangle of covers, articles of clothing littered the room. He sketchily smoothed the beds and hung the clothes on the wall pegs. And all the time his stomach felt peculiar on account of Tolly Mayhew looking at him from under her long blond bangs.

Tuck was glad to leave the house and feel the benign air about him again. Pete Degley's mood was not benign. His voice cracked like a whip over Tuck and Lily when their performance failed to meet his demands. "Anybody'd think you had six months to polish up in," he yelled, his face red and his steps jerky as he paced furiously about. He glared at them as if they were objects of disgust. "You're down to days now, every hour as precious as diamonds." He stopped pacing, put on his skates to illustrate his point, while Tuck stood by, panting and chagrined, feeling like the schoolboy of other years.

He did not know this Pete Degley. It was as if he had used up at last his seemingly inexhaustible supply of patience. He forgot all about Tolly Mayhew and her "poor old Tuck." There was no room in his head or his throbbing body for anything except the struggle for perfection Mr. Degley intended to exact at any cost. Tuck tried to emulate Lily's deadpan expression, certain he wasn't succeeding.

It was past noon when Pete blew his whistle to call them from the floor. "You're doing fine," he said shortly after a silence broken only by their hard breathing. "You're good, the both of you. Only thing wrong is, you're not good enough. I ought not to have to tell you that, but seeing I do, I can." A grin, surprising as sun bursting through the middle of a storm, broke the grimness of his leathery face. "Everybody starved as me?" He ruffled Lily's damp, clinging hair. "How about that chow you had 'em put up for us, girl?" He winked at Tuck. "Said it would cut in on our time too much to find a place to eat. Personally, I think she felt like a picnic, the day being like it is. Right, Lily girl?"

Lily, huddled on the bench, was tenderly rubbing a white-socked foot, the brown hair parting on her neck and falling on either side of her face. She straightened, wriggled her thin shoulders.

"Throw me my shoes, Pete. You eat with us, Tuck," she added, smiling at Tuck as she thrust her feet into scuffed moccasins. "There's enough sandwiches in that sack to feed an army." She tilted her face to sniff at the air drifting through the partly opened window. "Feels like spring today," she said. "And it nearly Christmas."

Pete's laughter echoed in the big building. "Didn't I tell you? A picnic's what she's after, Faraday. You know your way around these parts. Whereabouts could we be by ourselves to chow up, the three of us?"

"There's nobody up at the h-house," Tuck heard himself saying. "We could go up there." He was overcome at his impulsiveness. His father's "Howdy" to a neighboring farmer come to borrow, his stepmother's "Have a chair" to the rare woman visitor, were all he knew of hospitality. He had never brought anyone home from school with him. Now he had taken the plunge he felt sharp regret that he couldn't go whole hog, provide an abundant spread for them, be a proper host to these, his guests. "There's— There's plenty of trees," he said, shyly.

"Why don't we?" Lily cried, jumping up from the bench. "Won't anybody see us. Anyhow, what if they do! We won't be skating. I don't know when I've set foot in a real yard or been that close to a real house. I'm getting mighty tired of the Dixie Belle, even if it is the nicest motel around here."

"Looks like I'm going to have to get her a house if we stick around long as I think we will and business turns out like I look for it to," Pete said with a wink at Tuck. "Reckon I've worn out the gypsy in her. She couldn't get enough of wandering when she teamed up with this old vagabond, Faraday. Now, it's starting to stick in her craw." He lifted the large grocery bag along with Lily's jacket. "Put this on, hon. Don't want you catching cold. This mild weather's likely a weather breeder. Faraday, you get us some Co'-Cola out of the cooler."

Pete closed the window and locked the door. With a hammering heart Tuck led them through the orchard to the yard, Lily chattering like a kid let out of school, Pete chewing a twig and whistling. His hat rode the back of his head, his brown shoes with their morning shine twinkled in the brown leaves.

Ordinarily Tuck did not see the shabbiness, familiar to him as his arms or legs. Now, looking through Pete's and Lily's eyes, he saw his home for what it was: a down-at-the-heel, slipshod jumble of buildings looking as if they'd sprouted out of the eroded land. He caught the faint, acrid tang from the chicken house and dared not look at Lily, afraid he would see her little nose wrinkle with distaste. He couldn't imagine what had come over him, bringing them up here as if he had something to show off. . . .

"There's a good place," Lily cried, pointing to the giant oak fifty feet or so from the house, its twisted roots protruding from the sand-and-clay earth, its rusty leaves chuckling in the light wind. "Let's eat under that tree."

"We could eat on the p-porch," Tuck offered. He looked quickly away from the clutter on the porch: Karen's paper dolls, forgotten and left for the wind to scatter, a bucket turned upside down, Ida's scrub rags pinned to the clothesline strung between the posts. "W-We could go in the house," he added a little desperately, seeing them look round them, relaxed and dreamy.

"It's trees for me," Lily sang out, running toward the oak. She threw over her shoulder, "You boys can eat where you please," and sat herself down under the oak, hugging her knees.

Pete lifted a shoulder in comic helplessness. "That's it, Faraday. What can a man do when a woman gets a notion in her head?" He carried the bag to Lily and deposited it with a flourish at her feet. Tuck followed, vaguely unsatisfied with his efforts but warming to their lightness of heart.

Lily delved into the grocery bag, handed out packets of sandwiches wrapped in waxed paper. "You have to peep inside to see what kinds," she said, the gold ring on her finger glinting as she pushed her hair from her cheek. "I think I told them pimento and ham and roast beef."

Tuck saw what she meant by "enough for an army" and laughed with her when she said, "Tuck, I bet you never saw a guy eat as much as Pete and stay so skinny."

By the time the pile of sandwiches had diminished beyond belief all Tuck's uneasiness had ebbed away. He took the leftovers to the pigs, set a match to the wadded grocery sack and waxed paper and dropped them into the smoke-blackened oil drum that served as an incinerator. He wasn't about to leave anything lying around to raise suspicion; he still had an uneasy moment now and then about Karen.

"It sure is peaceful up here," Lily murmured drowsily,

her head cradled on her arm. "Like we were the only people in the world." She closed her eyes.

Pete sharpened an oak twig for a toothpick. "We've enjoyed your hospitality, Faraday," he said, gravely. "Thank you kindly."

Tuck blushed. "Aw, forget it, Mr. Degley. You-all f-furnished your own grub. That's not—" He stopped, afraid of getting hung up on the word hospitality.

Pete gave him a long, steady look. "If anybody is beholden, it's me. Most jobs, while a guy trains he gets paid. You have not seen one thin dime from me and I've worked you blind. You got a right to quit on me any time you get fed up, but you haven't and I don't worry that you will." He put the tips of his fingers together and squinted at them, thoughtfully.

"B-But we had a deal, Mr. Degley," Tuck protested, getting hot under the neck of his sweat shirt. "There wasn't anything about m-money in it. You told me that, yourself."

Pete nodded slowly, still studying the tips of his fingers. "Right. But maybe there ought to've been. Considering the time I've taken off of you." He looked round the yard. "I've a notion you haven't got a lot of spare time."

Tuck's throat clamped so hard he had to swallow; it was the first time that had happened, when he was with Pete and Lily, in some time, come to think of it. There was no way he could tell Pete Degley what the time had meant to him; he wasn't sure he knew himself. He had never thought of learning to skate as a job—and as to being paid for it, he would have laughed, it was so ridiculous, except for Mr. Degley's gravity. He looked cautiously at Pete and saw him looking down at Lily, his face, that could be so tough, wonderfully gentle. It made a lump in Tuck's throat.

"Sound asleep," Pete said. "And me fixing to put her to work again." He touched the end of her nose and her eyelids trembled. "Come on, little one. Time to get back to the rink."

Lily blinked, sat up and stretched, lithe as a cat.

"He's awful, Tucker," she said in a sleep-husky tone. "I married me a terrible man." She fell against him, laughing and yawning at the same time. "You shouldn't tangle with a man like him, I'm telling you. For your own good, too."

Tuck did not know how to participate in such child's play that was yet so different from the play of children. He stood on the edge of it, apart, pleased but embarrassed, relieved when Mr. Degley pulled her to her feet and gave her a playful slap on the dusty seat of her slacks.

Walking back to the rink, though, Tuck felt light-hearted from his exposure to the foolishness of Pete and Lily Degley. Even the unreasonable, fleeting pain he sometimes suffered at their tenderness with each other was a good pain, its yearning better than the drabness of his days before he knew them.

"What you want for Christmas, Tucker?" Lily asked as they came out of the orchard.

Tuck didn't know what to say. Christmas wasn't much at the Faradays'. When he and Tom and Clete were kids there had always been some little thing for each of them—a pocketknife, a whistle, a toy car or airplane from the five-and-ten. Such childishness had long since been put aside and now only their half sister Karen paid any attention to Christmas.

"Pair of shoes, I reckon," Tuck said, making a joke. But he caught himself thinking, Like Mr. Degley's. He thought Pete's shoes must be very expensive and he greatly admired the elegant shine of them.

Lily didn't return Tuck's grin. She looked at him, solemn and thoughtful. He had the idea, all of a sudden, that—before she was Mrs. Degley—Lily might have wanted a pair of shoes for Christmas and, so, saw nothing funny in it.

8

CHRISTMAS VACATION was over. Tuck went back to school. He had the curious feeling that only his body was there; his mind was at the rink. His preoccupation added to his previous difficulties, making him an object of ridicule on more than one occasion.

Miss Bayliss held up the whole English class to lecture him on his absent-mindedness, ending with a sour face, "Where *are* you, Tucker, anyway? Obviously not in this room." And when the usual guffaws and titters raced round the room, she looked rather pleased with herself instead of angry at the class as she used to.

Tuck reddened but looked straight in front of him, refusing to let on that he recognized Elva Grimes's high-pitched giggle above the others.

Mr. Buford, his science teacher, detained him after class to protest that his grades were sliding down the scale at an alarming rate. "You know how important your written assignments are, since you contribute very little otherwise. In the group—" He seemed to change his mind and didn't complete what he'd started to say, asking instead, "Have you given up homework altogether?"

Tuck gave him a shrug, looking sullenly past the teacher's worried face. "I might add for your benefit," Mr. Buford said in a tight voice, "that insolence won't make your position any better." Dismissed, Tuck wondered why he hadn't told Mr. Buford flat-out that it didn't make any difference about his grades, that he would only be in school till March. But even that didn't matter now; nothing mattered except to make Pete Degley proud of him on the night of January fifteenth.

The rink site was deserted now. No workmen, no yellow Chevrolet except at rehearsal hours. The tool shed had been disassembled and taken away, debris raked into piles and burned. The building stood, huge and naked, awaiting its hour. When Tuck came from school he did not linger but tramped steadily up the path to chores he did without having to think, his thoughts moving ahead of him to the evening's work.

"What are they waiting for?" Ida said, looking from the front room window at the rounded roof of the rink. "It's all done, ain't it?"

"Signs say January fifteen," Clete said, laying the Sears catalog on the table. "Reckon that opening's going to be something, all right. They say he's gonna have a girl come in from somewheres—up north, I guess—to do fancy skating."

Tuck, staring with unseeing eyes at the television screen,

stole a look at Karen. She slid her pale eyes at him and he barely moved his head in negation. She pulled her mouth in tight and, like Tuck, looked back at the TV screen.

Ida sniffed. "You can't tell nothing by what folks say. Maybe he's overextended hisself building such a big monster of a place like that. Must of cost plenty."

"Looks like he'd open it up and start taking in a little dough, then," Tom reasoned. He ran a pocket comb tenderly through his hair. "Ask old Tuck how come he's waiting so long to open. He oughta know all about it, way he's hobnobbed with that guy Degley."

When Tuck didn't turn his head, Tom went on. "They say Degley brings in a whole mess of people to work for him out of other places he's got. Somebody in town told Mr. Buddy Mayhew that. Say they're going to give lessons, Saturday mornings. Who'd pay out money to learn how to skate? I couldn't learn by myself, I wouldn't tell it." He laughed sneeringly. "You aiming to take lessons, Tuck?"

Tuck leaned toward the TV screen, gave no sign of having heard.

Ida sniffed again. "Looks like he'd give local people the chanct of a job if he's hiring help—I don't mean learning kids to skate. Must be other work if he's bringing in from outside like you say. But that's always the way with something like that coming in from nowheres—shows and carnivals and circuses. Take off of a community and give out nothing."

"They got a snack bar in there," Tom contributed. "I seen it when there wasn't nobody around and I looked in the window."

Tuck's heart began to race as Karen said in a superior tone, "You better not be peeping in no windows. They got No Trespassing signs up out there. Can't you read?" Tuck smiled at her as Tom dropped a brief invective too low for Ida's ears to catch.

"I know one thing," Tom said. "I'm gonna be at that opening, whatever it's like. Already got me a date with Tolly—" He glanced uncertainly at Cletus.

"Bully for you, boy," Clete retorted. "I got me a date, too. I'm not saying who, though." He pursed his mouth at the curiosity Tom was unable to keep out of his face. "You got you a date for the opening, Tuck?"

Tuck got up and stalked out, stopping in the hall, a feeling of indecision on him. Since Christmas the family had been as dreamlike as school, but the idle remarks of Ida and his brothers had penetrated the vacuum in which he moved. His stepmother's voice came through the thin wood of the door. "You ought to be ashamed of yourself, picking on your brother like you do, Clete Faraday. He's liable to surprise you one of these days. Still water runs deep, they say, and your brother's a still one."

"You can't start no argument thataway," Clete said, bringing a guffaw from Tom and a giggle from Karen.

"Mr. Degley is Tuck's friend," Karen piped. "He told me so hisself. Right here in this room."

"What was Mr. Degley doing in this room?" Clete demanded, feigning shocked surprise.

Standing outside the door, Tuck licked his dry lips. What else was Karen going to say? He heard the note of fury in her answer: "Not him, *Tuck*." She couldn't bear much teasing without falling apart, though she was a master hand at it herself.

Ida yelled suddenly, "You-all cut out that fool carrying on right now. If there was a one of you worth your salt you'd find something to do 'stead of picking at one another. At Tuck, specially. The Lord give him a cross to carry and maybe we were all meant to learn a little patience from it. You come set the table for me, Karen, and you boys get out there and help your daddy. Don't anybody but Tuck give him a hand without you're drove to. Maybe he could of made out better with his projects if he'd of been helped more."

Tuck moved away from the door, mingled feelings of doubt, irritation, and a sulky sort of gratitude tearing at him. Doubt of Karen's ability to keep her knowledge of his coming performance to herself if the twins continued to bait her, irritation at his stepmother's persistent defense of him and, most dismaying of all, gratitude toward her at the same time the old irritation stung him like a cloud of gnats.

He tried to shake his mind free of such petty considerations; he had more important things to occupy it, goodness knew. But the feelings kept troubling him off and on all the next day at school. Without ever really making up his mind to, he found himself going down the main street after school instead of toward the old part of town and his shorter way home. He cut through the alley behind the SPOTLESS DRYCLEANERS to Burl Wilson's secondhand shop.

A long time ago—it must have been right after the Faradays moved to Wesley—Tuck had sneaked to the dark little hole-in-the-wall to look at bicycles. If he remembered correctly there had been two or three electric stoves standing among rusted bedsteads and battered chairs.

There was, of course, no point in his return to the shop—there had been no point in his looking at bicycles, either—but he was certain a secondhand electric stove wouldn't cost anything like what the TV set had, and his father had been persuaded to buy that. Tuck remembered Karen bawling because everybody but the Faradays had a TV and Ida backing her up. Even Tom and Clete had promised handsomely to contribute to the payments when they got work. Only Tuck had remained silent. The funny part was that Tuck's father had looked as proud as any of them when the Faraday roof sprouted its antenna along with all the other roofs.

Burl Wilson spat a brown stream of tobacco juice into the alley and smiled slyly at Tuck. "You aiming to get married and set up housekeeping, young feller?"

Tuck ignored the question, standing off and looking with speculative eyes at a stove that looked less sad than the other two. It was large and reasonably clean, its color pale pink. Burl offered to plug it in and show Tuck that it worked.

"Wasn't nothing much wrong with it. One burner had give out and I replaced it and cleaned 'er up nice like you see 'er there. Old lady Bradley got her a new range off Sears. They don't take trade-ins and I give her forty-five bucks for this one. I'll let 'er go for sixty. That new burner cost me eighteen bucks, so you can see I'm losing like it is, but I need the room."

Tuck didn't believe any of Burl's figures were correct,

but he didn't bat an eye. He didn't know why he was wasting his time, anyway. It was silly and he felt like kicking himself. He devoutly hoped nobody would come along and catch him looking at cook stoves after Burl Wilson's crack. He hung around a little longer, picking up and putting down a hoe with a spliced handle, a rusty rifle, two books whose titles he didn't read, seeing only the curled soft covers and the dust on them.

"Better let me make you a deal on this range, mister," Burl said but without enthusiasm.

"I was just l-looking," Tuck muttered, edging toward the door.

Once he was around the corner and back on Main Street Tuck walked briskly, wanting to make up his lost time. In the vacant lot next to the supermarket one of Pete Degley's signs proclaimed in red letters nearly a foot high the opening of the ELYSIUM ON WHEELS. Some little kids were skating in front of The People's Bank and Trust Company. Tuck hurried along the street, feeling January fifteenth crowding, pressing in on him. He was glad to leave the shabby stores and the town behind him, but even in the country space and quiet a sense of time running out followed him.

In the orchard the bare peach trees looked squat and black. Dead leaves lay curled on the ground, the late wintry sun casting thin, lacy shadows on them. Overhead a gray cloud moved in a wind too high up and light to feel. The silence of the rink behind him made Tuck hunch his wide shoulders against a thing he could not name. Maybe the best days were over, the days when he had followed Pete

Degley round the site, watching the building, feeling the gradual unfolding of something new and good within himself.

Up at the house Myron was putting a new fence round the garden patch he hoped to plow next month—or the next. With a start, Tuck realized that March and his sixteenth birthday were not so far away. He tried to feel exultation—but nothing happened. He was going to quit school, going to be one of the dropouts everybody heard so much about. So what. He would be rid of all the torments school had brought him, but his feeling was still: So what. There was nothing beyond January fifteenth, a little more than a week away.

He changed his clothes and went to help his father with the fence. Myron's thin gray hair wisped from under his stained old hat, the faded overalls hung on his spare form. Wonder how old Pa is, Tuck thought. Maybe no older than Mr. Degley, yet he never thought of Pete as old and he always thought so of his father. He banged a nail into a post, stretched wire with cold fingers. He carried water for the chickens, fed them, went in at last to the warmth of the kitchen.

Watching his stepmother dragging her feet on the journeys from stove to table to sink, Tuck thought of Burl Wilson's dingy little shop and tried to picture the pink stove in place of the old squat-legged iron thing Ida hated with such a passion. But his imagination didn't seem to be working; he couldn't see the kitchen other than it was now and had been all the years he'd been in and out of it.

When he had bolted his food, Tuck went into the bedroom and lay down on his narrow bed. There was no heat in the room and he pulled the quilt over him. Added to his mounting dread of opening night was a queer feeling of regret—for his father, for his stepmother and his brothers, for the foolish squabblings and meaningless laughter hiding things that never came out into the light. He never used to have such thoughts. Family was family, that was all. You endured what you had to from them and accepted it with other inconveniences—all as familiar as your own face. Family wasn't like school that you could quit when you were sixteen.

Tom came in, blundered for the string hanging from the bulb, and plunged the room into painful light. Tuck flung his arm over his face.

"You sick or something?" Unwelcome as the light, Tom's question jarred Tuck.

"Nope."

"You going out after a while?"

Tuck did not answer. Why did they have to start probing and prodding now, after all this time?

"You go out ever' night, don't you?"

Tuck made no sign that he heard.

"Know what I b'lieve, Tuck boy? I have come to the conclusion that you've got a girl hid out somewheres."

Couldn't they ever think of anything but girls? Tuck wanted to leap from the bed and strike Tom. He had to force himself to remain motionless while Tom went on, enjoying himself hugely. "Only thing is, I can't figure out who she could be. Or where she lives at. Must be some little old gal don't go to school. I'd know if it was anybody down there at Wesley school. Clete and me would know that, all right."

Ida's scream brought Tuck from the bed in the leap he had not made for Tom. Karen's wail came on the heels of it, then a shout from Cletus. Tuck and Tom reached the kitchen at the same instant, wild-eyed, mouths agape.

Ida and Karen cowered between the table and the wall, howls issuing steadily from their wide-open mouths. Cletus was at the sink, trying to fill a bucket from the tap, but the pressure was weak and the water flowed in a feeble stream, rising with hopeless slowness in the tin milk bucket. Myron, in his gray woolen undershirt, was beside the stove, beating at the pipe with his blue work shirt. Soot fell in wooly clouds about him and tongues of orange flame spurted from a widening crack in the stovepipe near the ceiling.

Tom ripped his shirt off, buttons flying to bounce and roll on the floor. With his father he struck at the pipe, half his blows catching Myron who still made no sound in the bedlam already reigning. Tuck, unable to think of anything original, tore his shirt off, too, and ran round the stove to thrash at the split pipe from the rear. Clete snatched the half-filled pail from the sink and heaved its contents toward the stove. Tom yelled as the icy water struck him and spattered on the stove to hiss and steam.

Tuck felt laughter welling in him, uncontrollable, lung-bursting. He let it go, tears rolling down his face as he gasped and choked on his untimely mirth. In the wild confusion nobody noticed, or else laid it to the smoke, and Tuck had the grace to be glad. It was all over in seconds, anyway. Smoke fogged the kitchen, soot covered floor, table, chairs, and Myron's face. Tuck's laughter went as suddenly as it had come. Karen howled louder, now that Ida had stopped; the twins swore loudly and in unison. "That'll do, boys," Myron panted. "Fire's out."

Tuck tracked through the soot to open the door; his father raised the window. Turning from the door, Tuck saw his stepmother's face and shame for his laughter filled him. Ida's tears ran like rain from her smoke-reddened eyes, made tracks down her grimed face. Her head swung slowly from side to side like that of a tormented bull. She pointed a shaking finger at the stove that was still steaming faintly, its flue listing crazily to one side.

"Look," she sobbed. "Look at that! That's what I got to cook your vittles on."

Myron began to wash at the sink. He soaped and scrubbed his face, reached for the towel. "Have to get a new piece of pipe," he said and Ida collapsed onto a chair, crying wildly. Myron turned on Karen who was still howling. "You hush that racket," he stormed. "Now, you hush up. Can't you see how bad your mama feels without you calling down the country with your bawling?"

Tuck stepped out the open door into the chilly darkness. He could not imagine what had struck him funny. Compared to Ida's grief, Tom's drenching seemed scarcely worth a smile. He went round the house, slipped in at the front door, and took his shower while the others were still creating a commotion in the kitchen. He put on his clothes and went down to the rink.

From the orchard he saw the thin cracks of light round the tarpaulins Pete draped over the windows against curious eyes and knew Pete and Lily were there. It was not till he had closed the heavy door behind him that he stopped seeing Ida's soot-grimed, tear-tracked face—as if he had left it out there in the dark with the door between it and the music-filled world of the rink.

9

❁❁❁❁❁❁❁❁

ALL THAT last week fear was Tuck's companion. Only during rehearsals was he without its cold presence; skating, he had no thought of it or of anything other than what he was doing. But when he crept between his chilly sheets and lay, staring into the darkness, hearing the heavy, adenoidal breathing of Tom and the sporadic snorts of Cletus, fear moved in on him. He counted the days, the hours, till he would be out there, prey once more to scornful eyes, to jeers and laughter.

Why had he ever thought it could be anything but the terrible culmination of all he had suffered? He hadn't thought, that was it; he had but blindly followed Pete Degley's leading. He'd been a kid, dazzled by a kid's hero-worship. Why had he let it get this far before he realized, woke up to what it was bound to be? He couldn't run out on Mr. Degley now—or could he? Maybe if he struck out up the highway after Pete and Lily had gone to the Dixie

Belle Motel and the Faradays slept, unsuspecting, uncaring . . .

But he wouldn't do that, he couldn't do that to Mr. Degley. Never mind why not, why didn't matter. He simply knew that he couldn't do it. He would have to go through with it now. If he couldn't remember a move when the hour came, if his legs became paralyzed and he fell flat on his face, giving Wesley and the countryside and surrounding towns the biggest laugh they'd ever had, he'd have to go through with it.

Twice, that week, he had the nightmare of his childhood, a little changed now but no less terrifying. When the muddy waters of the pond rose, instead of trying to call out, he would suddenly cease to be the little kid watching his mother drown and become the six-footer he was in reality. He would turn his face from the swollen pond and skate away, faster and faster with a terrible momentum he could do nothing about, his feet winged, taking him away from the tragedy that had etched the pattern for his youth and made the world he had known. But in the dream there was no elation, no sense of escape or triumph. There was only the heavy knowledge of what he had fled, following him, trying to pull him back. He would wake in a cold sweat, his heart pounding till his ribs ached, his body trembling violently.

At school there was constant talk of the opening, and to escape it Tuck stayed more to himself than ever. It never occurred to him to speak of his distress to Mr. Degley or Lily. He would have been bitterly ashamed to let either of them know he'd turned chicken. At home he watched the family going their appointed ways, unknowing, unchanged—and the certainty that he had inherited his father's matchless talent for failure would clammily enfold him.

Ida Faraday had cleared away the last remnant of the disaster and the kitchen was cleaner than Tuck had ever seen it. Tom and Clete promised to paint it, come spring. Tuck heard the blithe promise, but was too miserable to smile. The old stove had a shiny new length of pipe that Myron declared safe, and though Ida glared at it with hatred she did not once mention an electric stove. Tuck knew she had given up, as his father so often gave up. Tuck's moments in Burl Wilson's secondhand shop were as if they had never been. More than half ashamed of that stealthy visit, he was willing to forget it. To struggle through the hours between skating seemed all that he could manage. They were so few now, and growing fewer, closing in upon him, coming to the final trap beyond which lay nothing.

"Don't you feel good, Tuck?" Lily asked once. "You're kind of white around the gills."

Pete Degley raked Tuck's face with a sharp look. "Don't you go getting the flu on me, man," he said. "There's always plenty of it around this time of year."

"I'm O.K.," Tuck mumbled, swallowing at the dry spot that was always in his throat these days. Pete laid a hand on Tuck's shoulder.

"You're going to be all right, Faraday. Have I ever lied to you?" His look held Tuck's eyes. "I couldn't work with a man long as I have with you and not know him—and what he can do." It helped for a moment. But the fear came back.

On Wednesday of that week Tuck was late getting home from school. His need for escape and peace had driven him to the pine woods beside the creek. He had avoided the place since the day Elva Grimes went there with him. He stopped for a few moments to breathe the pungent scent of pine needles. It was another of those deceptive days after the rawness since Christmas, hinting of a spring not yet ready but teasing to stir the longing for it. He passed the mound where he and Elva had sat and a smile that was not really a smile twisted his face and was gone. He stood on the creek bank and stared at the brown water. Mellow bugs darted on its surface; little gray minnows clustered at the base of a rock.

Tuck cast the press of time from him and dawdled as if he were carefree. When he reached the farm Tom and Cletus had not showed up either, though the school bus had long since passed. He entered the chicken house and saw three drooping hens gasping through parted beaks, eyes filmed, heads slightly swollen.

Myron Faraday rose from squatting beside their boxes. His eyes sparked anger as he hooked his knotted hands in the straps of his overalls and confronted Tuck. "How come you just now hauling in here? I don't get you, boy, I don't know what you been up to all this fall, but I know it ain't good. A boy goes and comes without a word to anybody, even if he does make out he can't talk, he's up to some kind of devilment."

Staring at him, Tuck could only think how old he looked, old and pitiful. That's what his father was, a pitiful old man. I used to think I needed him, Tuck thought. Well,

I don't. Maybe it's the other way round. Maybe he needs me—

"I'm getting fed up with it, you hear me?" Myron ranted on, his voice getting thinner as it rose. "Your brothers have done got too big for their britches and now you're gettin' the same idea. Well, you might be too big for me to whup, but I'm boss here and you better recollect it ever' now and then. Come wandering in here like you got all the time in the world. My chickens are dying on me—" The angry tone shifted to whining. He jerked his hand toward the boxes. "Them three since morning. I don't know what went with that medicine you used for the last lot. You don't ever give out a word. It's like you hold yourself too good for your own folks in your own home where you still put your feet under the table."

Tuck squatted beside the boxes and took one of the sick hens, holding it under his arm. He looked sharply at the swelling head, drew a finger gently over it. "I'll see to 'em," he said quietly.

"About time," Myron sputtered, trying, Tuck could tell, to call his anger back but making a poor job of it. "It's coming on dusk-dark. I can't count on anybody around here. Not even you that can't do nothing else but help with chores."

Tuck, starting for the barn where he had left the little bottle of drops last time, stopped. He looked down from his full height at his father.

"You want me to doctor these hens or don't you?" His voice was strange to him—one he had never used to his father. Myron scraped his feet uncertainly, his sharp face pinched with something more like grief than rage. Tuck hardened himself against it, whatever it was. "Well, do you?" he demanded. "All you got to do is s-say so if you want me to g-get out."

"Get that medicine and quit shootin' off your face," Myron grumbled. "Anybody want a word out of you and you make like you're struck dumb. You can speak up when you take the notion, I see."

Tuck administered drops to each of the three hens, holding them firmly, making soft clucking noises to them, neither asking nor receiving help from his father. Myron wandered off to busy himself with bucket and feed sack. Tuck stroked the sick hens gently, murmuring to them, letting his stored tenderness out freely with no one to see and jeer at him. If the sickness spread it would be disastrous, but that thought touched only the edge of his mind. He made three trips to take the boxes, one by one, to the moldy-smelling little half-basement under the kitchen.

"Lookit them pants," Ida exclaimed when he went into the kitchen. "Full of fuzz—and what's that brown stuff on your shirt? I vow, Tuck Faraday, you must be nutty as a fruit cake. Why didn't you change out of your good clothes for chores? I can't fathom you, these days."

"You got any croup salve?" Tuck brushed at his trousers without looking at them.

"Bathroom cupboard," Ida answered, folding her ironing board and thrusting it behind the food safe. "Why? You got a cold coming on you?"

Tuck shook his head. When he came back through the kitchen with the jar of dark, creosote-smelling salve Ida screeched, "You going to give them hens human's medicine?" She looked undecided whether to laugh or berate him.

As he knelt in the basement, Tuck heard her clumping down the narrow steps, puffing and grumbling. He didn't look round but went on lighting the little kerosene stoves used to keep the chickens' water from freezing in extremely cold weather. He dropped a generous lump of the sticky salve in each of the three coffee cans of water and placed them on the tiny stoves, turning the flames as high as they would go. He draped burlap sacks over each of the boxes, making tents to hold the steam, careful to keep the cloth from touching the flames.

"The old house didn't burn down last time, so you aim to finish it off now, I reckon," Ida observed, hands on hips. Tuck said nothing. "I bet it'll be like two years ago," she went on, grimly, "Half of 'em dyin' off. Funny these takened down just when the weather's turned pretty after all that cold. Guess they'd already commenced to sicken. Croup salve!" She gave a sudden squawk of laughter. "Wonder you don't rub their chest with it. Like I used to rub yours when you was little and croupy."

Karen called from somewhere in the house and Ida called back, "Down here, sugar. You stay up there. Don't come down here in this old dugout."

Tuck heard Karen's voice going on and on, petulantly, then his father's steps going into the house.

"Reckon I got to start supper," Ida sighed. Her felt slippers dragged over the rough dirt floor of the basement.

Tuck did not sit down with the others, though his stepmother urged him, giving him the old stuff about growing boys needing to keep their strength up. Tuck said he had homework and shut himself into the bedroom. The scrape of knives and forks on plates, the rise and fall of Ida's voice, the jets of talk from Tom and Clete, and the whine of Karen floated through his head. Then he heard his father say, "Reckon Tuck's sulling. I give him the edge of my tongue when he come draggin' in a hour late."

"How come Tuck's always the one to get the edge of your tongue?" Ida came back. "Looks like he's not the only one's late around here."

Tuck clenched his hands. Why did she always have to say something in his behalf? Let the old man brag if it did anything for him. Then he heard Clete's voice. "Me and Tom stopped at the station. Yancy wants us Saturday morning. Reckon he figures cars'll be filling up to go to the rink opening. Grand opening. Wonder that place hasn't rotted down, waiting to open. Something's been going on in there quite a while, though. Couple from Fidelia tried to look in but the doors was locked and the windows covered up. Said there was skating in there, though. They could hear it. Reckon it was some of those folks Degley's got working for him."

"I wouldn't put no dependency in what folks say," Ida said contemptuously. "They will run off at the mouth, no matter what. Truth's something else."

"I'm going to the opening," Karen announced, fierceness replacing her habitual plaintiveness. "I might could take lessons and learn to skate like the girls I saw on TV."

"You might could," Tom drawled. "I might could go

up in the next space rocket, too, and come back alive to tell what I saw."

"That was ice skating on TV," Cletus reminded Karen. "It's harder than roller skating. Anybody can roller-skate."

Tuck stirred, uneasy as always at the exchange between Karen and his brothers. Trying not to hear them, he fixed his mind on his father, silent since his brief attempt at self-assertion. Myron was almost as apart from the others as Tuck himself. They didn't pay any mind to what he had to say, Tuck thought. They don't ever pay him any mind. That could sort of turn a man sour, I reckon. It was a thought that had never occurred to Tuck before. Things always seemed to be coming through to him now—as if a light had come on where it had been dark before. As if his family had become people instead of just family.

He saw a star prick through the dark blue of the evening sky, then another. Soon he would be out there on the floor, skating with Lily, and family would be forgotten—family and bad dreams and the dread riding him. He rubbed his hands together, damp palms sticking. Maybe that's the way it would be on opening night. Maybe he would only need to hear that part of "Swan Lake" and nothing in his life would ever have been and nothing more would ever be except skating.

He went softly down the hall and out the front door, round to the basement steps. The tiny underground room was filled with the pungent scent of croup salve. He found the light cord and pulled it. He opened the burlap sacking at the tops of the boxes and looked in. The hens nestled, motionless, but one of them had her beak closed and her eyes shut. Encouraged, Tuck arranged the tents again, added a little water to the coffee cans, adjusted the flames of the stoves. He looked round the dreary little room, at the cobwebbed window pane, the dirt floor, the cartons and barrels pushed into a corner, a broken rocking chair, a fragment of iron bedstead. He turned the light out and groped his way up the rickety steps.

For no particular reason Tuck went to the kitchen window and looked in. The family were still at the table, the twins leaning back in their chairs, Ida propped on both elbows, the inevitable lock of hair hanging on her cheek. His father was reading the paper, moving his thin lips over the words.

Tuck turned away and started toward the orchard. It was too early for Pete and Lily to be at the rink, but never mind. He would wait for them there.

10

THE FIFTEENTH of January dawned in mizzling rain, harried by mean bursts of wind. The wet cold seeped through Tuck's clothing as he did his morning chores, edged his brothers' arguing with ill humor. Karen snuffled and whined with a cold in her head, and her mother said she could not go out if it wasn't better by evening. Clete and Tom gobbled the breakfast Ida set before them and went down to the highway to hitch a ride to town.

The day crawled by, going too fast even so, bringing Tuck's ordeal closer with every tick of the greasy-faced clock. The house was bursting with family but its discord rose and fell about Tuck without touching him.

At supper Ida tried to coax Karen out of going to the opening.

"I ab goi'd," Karen muttered on the heels of a sneeze and her father shouted to her to mind her tongue or she'd be going to bed.

"You go down there with a lotta riffraff, you're liable to catch wors'n a cold," Ida wheedled. "That rink'll be there when you're shut of your cold. You stay home with me and we'll make us some syrup candy to pull."

"I doe wadda pull doe caddy," Karen wailed, casting a look of desperation at Tuck. "It's the *opening,* Ma." She stopped short, blew her nose loudly and added, "I wadda skate."

"Fat lot you know about skating," Tom scoffed.

"Tuck might could teach you," Clete suggested. "All the time he's spent round there he must be a expert."

Karen, red-faced, started to make a retort and Tuck pushed his chair back from the table, noisily. They all looked at him but he looked only at Karen, as if the others weren't there. She pressed her lips sullenly together, her red face looking ready to burst. Passing her chair, Tuck put his hand on the back of her neck a second and Karen stuck her tongue out at Clete instead of speaking.

Tuck washed and dressed hurriedly so he could go down to the rink ahead of the others. He put on a clean shirt and jeans and combed his hair as carefully as if he were Tom or Cletus. There was no real reason for him to get there early. But, apart from feeling that he must go alone, as always, he hoped to find, somehow, in the atmosphere of the rink the courage that seemed all week to have been dwindling.

At the rink, he stood looking about him. All was bustle and strangeness. Behind the cash register was a brassy-haired, stoutish woman. At the snack bar, now amply stocked with the delicacies dear to the stomachs of teen-agers, was a young man in a wild plaid shirt. A spotty-faced boy with hair longer than Tom's checked skate sizes. So it was true that Pete Degley had brought his staff in from outside Wesley. Tuck had never laid eyes on any of them before. The fact that he alone had been chosen from the local scene held only added terror for him at the moment.

Even Pete, whipping about with an air of being everywhere at once, might have been someone Tuck had never seen before. Lily was nowhere in sight. Tuck stiffened his knees against their weak trembles and moved in front of the empty spectators' benches toward the cubicle in the rear where he was to change his clothes.

His costume hung against the wall: white tights and the scarlet shirt Lily had made and said she would press after the dress rehearsal, last night. Tuck touched a satin sleeve tenderly, then scowled at himself in the rectangle of mirror fastened to the door. He could hear Lily moving about on the other side of the thin partition and would have liked to smile at her needing so much more time than he for dressing—in such little scraps of a costume, too!—but he couldn't make the stiff muscles of his face give.

Tuck's and Lily's number was not to be till just before closing time. No use sweating his fancy rig up in this little cell of a dressing room. He felt the need of air and went out the rear door of the building to walk up and down behind it, sucking in the cold, wet air. A car turned off the highway into the parking area, then another and another. They were coming early enough! Doors slammed, young voices shrilled, headlights swung in bright arcs against the side of the building.

"Tuck? Tucker Faraday—" Lily's voice penetrated his mounting terror. He saw her coming toward him through the damp and dark. She had a white cape over her tight-fitting bodice and little bob-tailed skirt of fiery fish scales and she made Tuck think of a big light moth—the kind that blunder into the house on a summer night. "Oh, here you are. Got the jitters? I always have them, too, many times as I've been on with Pete. They don't mean a thing. In fact, Pete says they're a healthy sign." He felt her hand clutch his, icy but as steady as a rock.

Tuck gulped, "I'm O.K."

Lily pulled the cape round her arms, shivering. "We better go inside. I take cold easy, and you know what Pete's like when I do."

Inside the rink again, Tuck left Lily and made his way toward the front of the building. He pressed himself against the wall beside the bulletin board that announced skating lessons Saturday mornings ten to twelve. He saw Pete Degley and the spotted boy handing out skates as fast as the brassy-haired cashier could ring up admissions. There were almost as many older people on the spectators' seats as there were young ones reaching for skates. Some of those who were unwilling to risk life and limb but had come for the excitement of watching others do so were already rushing the snack bar, keeping the bright-shirted fellow on the jump.

Tuck saw his father and his stepmother sitting near the door and thought his father had selected a place handy to an exit should the evening prove too great a bore. Let him go, who cared? Tuck had not expected him to show up, anyway. He had not spoken directly to Tuck since the outburst three days ago, though two of the three ailing hens had recovered and no others had sickened.

A piercing whistle blast brought all eyes to Pete Degley in the center of the rink. He was on skates and a grin split his face. His voice rang out after the whistle, folksy and full of good salesmanship. Wonder at this Pete Degley battled with Tuck's stage fright, making him miss much of what Pete was saying. It came in waves and fragments to his ears, mostly nonsense, but he could see the crowd was lapping it up and loving it.

". . . want you all to have a good time tonight. . . . few regulations to keep in mind. . . . don't want anybody to get hurt—see you forgot to bring your sofa pillows to fasten on behind. . . ." Laughter, boisterous and wholehearted. "When this whistle sounds"—he held the police whistle on its cord around his neck for them to get a good look—"you all want to pull up and stop like a traffic cop was on your tail." More laughter. "When it blows next, you that's ready to roll fall in line and come onto the floor *through the break in the railing*. No scrounging or pushing under if you don't want to sit out the first round." A pause for this to sink in. "I repeat: We don't want anybody hurt. You big kids watch out for the little ones, and you limber young folks watch out for us oldsters that's brittle in the bones." Laughter, a few brash remarks and catcalls from bold local teen-agers.

The whistle shrilled, Pete began to skate backwards, his eyes everywhere. The "Glowworm," though amplified almost beyond bearing, failed to drown out completely the thump and slide of wheels on novice feet. The floor filled, the spills began. Pete Degley whipped in and out among the strugglers, each hand picking a child from the floor.

Tuck saw Karen shuffling along laboriously, one hand gripping the rail, the other making frequent dabs at her troublesome nose. Link Grover glided smoothly past in the inner circle to which Pete was directing the better skaters, Jenny Morrow clinging proudly to his arm. Tuck saw other boys and girls he knew, some skating in pairs, some singly. Most did better than he had in the beginning, but not all. He knew Pete would count on the poor skaters as candidates for instruction—the instruction with which Tuck was to help him. Pete had told him this only a few days ago when he put the bulletin up.

Flattening himself against the wall, Tuck thought how crazy it all was that he was a part of this—or would be if he didn't flub up the works tonight. Nerves twitched in his legs, making them feel weak. The shortness of his breath made him wonder if he might give out of wind and collapse. He imagined himself lying on the floor, gasping like a fish while the crowd hissed and booed and Pete Degley's dream died a shameful death.

Shaking his head to clear his vision, he had a fleeting glimpse of Tom and Tolly Mayhew, managing to keep on their feet but little more than that. Some experts from beyond Wesley were doing a little showing off—as much as the crowded floor permitted—and Tuck thought how strange it was that Mr. Degley had picked a raw country boy like himself to make into a skater. An artiste, as he always said so proudly. Fright deepened his humility and he wished Pete *had* chosen someone else—that guy out there with the blond hair swept carefully back above his sports collar.

Mr. Degley could have trained someone like that and saved himself a lot of bother along with Tuck Faraday's present anguish.

Then Tuck saw his brother Cletus and a yellow-headed girl and knew it was Elva Grimes before he saw her face. She was keeping Cletus on his feet by sheer, dogged effort, her shapely legs working stolidly and her hands bracing her unsteady partner.

As they came opposite Tuck, Clete's glazed look strayed from its hazardous course to his brother flattened against the wall. A grin broke the rigid surface of Clete's face. He pulled his hand from Elva's grasp and waved, shouting, "Hey, Tuck! Come on in, the water's fine." It was more than Elva could handle. Clete's feet flew from under him and down he went, pulling Elva on top of him. Her little quilted skirt flew up and her snug red panties showed to the waist.

The tension flowed out of Tuck as if a plug had been pulled to release it. As if he had waited only for this to happen he turned, slipped past the seat full of spectators, and shut himself into his dressing room. He sat on the one straight chair and let his thoughts tumble from one thing to another, random and inconsequential. The noise outside beat futilely against his ears, having nothing to do with him. After the anguished week, his relief was like sudden freedom from physical pain. He sat there a long while before he put his costume on, not feeling foolish as he had last night—like something escaped from the circus.

Pete Degley thumped on the door once and thrust his head in, his face agleam with perspiration. "You O.K., Faraday?"

"Yes, sir."

"I better send Lily in to make you up a little. I got to get back to see none of those kids bust themselves up." Tuck noticed Pete walked a little one-sided, favoring his bad leg.

Lily stood on tiptoe to darken Tuck's eyebrows and elongate the corners of his eyes. She put a little rouge on his cheeks and reddened his lips. Tuck burned with shame and dared not meet his reflection in the glass. She said, impatiently, "You got to have make-up to beat that spot. You'll look green, otherwise. How's your nerve?"

Tuck smiled, not wanting to waste himself on talk. But he was no longer afraid. Even when he heard Pete Degley's whistle bring the skaters to a grinding, thumping halt and the hubbub ebbed to comparative silence, he was not afraid.

"And now, ladies and gentlemen," Pete Degley's hoarse but strident voice announced, "I give you that bright Star of the Evening, Queen of Roller Skating, LILY. And her supporting star—TUCKER HOLLAND FARADAY."

The gasp from Wesleyans, shot through by one raucous bray of laughter, died as Tuck and Lily skated into the rink. The strains of Tchaikovsky's "Swan Lake" flowed into the stillness, the lights went down, the spotlight bloomed out of the dark to catch the glitter of sequins on Lily's skirt and the circlet round the smooth knob of hair on the top of her head. Tuck saw their flashing, nothing else. He felt nothing, neither the magic transmitted from the music to his body nor the breathless unbelief of the spectators.

Tuck and Lily circled the rink twice, their motion as of one skater. Tuck had no awareness of Lily's cold little hands in his; they were part of him, as he was part of the act. He saw her spinning round and round in the center of the rink, the spotlight on her like a heatless sun. He could not have counted the times they had gone through each part of the act Pete had so painstakingly choreographed, so relentlessly driven them to perfect. All that lay behind him, the moment was now—his moment and Pete Degley's.

His eyes on Lily's little flashing head, Tuck did not feel the elation building within him, giving lift to his feet, power to his body. They came together, they parted, they performed in a silence somehow more powerful than the sound of the music and the roll of their skate wheels, what they had performed those countless times to Pete Degley's furious shouts and peremptory orders to halt and begin again.

No doubt he was out there in the audience somewhere, watching. But he did not exist for Tuck, moving only in the magic circle of the spotlight, unaware of the darkened jungle of eyes.

There was not a sound from the audience till Tuck lifted Lily and swung her at the level of his outstretched arms, unconsciously counting the bars, gradually lowering her till her feet touched the floor and she was skating again beside him. Howls, cheers, stamping, and madly crackling palms brought Tuck to himself.

When the overhead lights sprang on and he saw the faces his numbness continued for a second, then feeling poured through him. He felt like God. As if nothing ever again would be beyond his grasp. They were pounding and screaming for more—those who had ridiculed him year after dreary year. His awareness sharpened to an ecstasy that was almost pain. He had done it. He, Tucker Holland Faraday. He had made Mr. Degley's dream come true.

Somehow, Tuck and Lily stood in the dim passage between the rink and the dressing rooms, their hard breathing slowing, settling to normal. Tuck could hear Pete's voice announcing that it was closing time, then the babble of talk, the shuffle of feet. He didn't know what the talk was and didn't care. It was done. A faint shadow of regret touched his ecstasy as he wondered if there could ever again be a moment to equal those just passed—moments swept already into time gone and behind him.

"You did it, Tucker," Lily said softly and he looked down to see her eyes shining up at him—as if she had had no part in it, as if it were all his show. Shame licked at him, for hadn't he been thinking the same?

"It—You did it, Lily. You were the s-star." The stammer irked him and he said it over, more carefully. "You were the star."

She shook her head, raised both hands and wiped her forehead. Something childlike in the gesture moved him. "I never did as well before. Not even when I skated with Pete. He'll tell you, you'll see. He knew you could do it and so did I." She shivered in the drafty passage. "See you later," she said and went into her dressing room.

Tuck was standing in his dressing room, still bemused, when Pete Degley hurried in. "Well, you pulled it off, Faraday. Not but what I knew you would. Still, I don't know but what you did a better job than I expected—and that's saying a mouthful! Congratulations, man. You're in now. You know that, don't you?"

Tuck shook his head. "It—It was you, Mr. Degley. You and—"

"Say, don't you think it's about time you dropped that 'mister,' Faraday? Pete's the name. We been through enough together that you've earned the right, I'd say." But the Pete did not come that easily to Tuck; his respect was too nearly reverence. "That crowd out there," Pete went on, "they never seen anything like this, you bet your life. You coulda heard a pin drop if it hadn't been for the music, I swear. You better get into dry clothes. I'll see you later."

He started out the door, then turned, grinning again. "Looks to me like this calls for a little celebration. How about the three of us going out after I get done here? Maybe find a place and dance some—if ever'thing's not rolled up and put away for the night."

Dance? Him? Tuck felt a blush crawling over his face. How did he know he couldn't? A short time ago he hadn't been able to skate. . . . Then—he didn't quite know why—he was shaking his head.

"No, Mr. Degley. Th-thanks just the same. I better get home. It'll be late—"

"Maybe you're right," Pete agreed. "Guess you're mighty near bushed as I am, young as you are. Well, take a rain check on it—and see me in the office, O.K.?" He walked out and Tuck saw that he was limping badly.

Tuck changed slowly, tending to fall into reverie, his shirt hanging from his hands, his eyes vacantly on the costume still damp from the heat of his body, hanging neatly on the wall. It had been a night; to prolong it would be a mistake. Besides, he felt the house above the orchard pulling at him, a thing he'd never felt before. . . .

Cars were still waiting their chance to get out onto

the highway, honking horns. Voices called, laughter rode the damp air. It did not strike Tuck as strange that none of his family had attempted to seek him out, congratulate him; in their place, he wouldn't have ventured behind the scene, either, he thought. And good old Karen, she had kept the secret. He bet she would run her tongue ragged, now that it was over. He could just imagine her at school. And what a time she'd give Tom and Clete. He chuckled, slipping his shirt on over chilling shoulders.

11

THE CROWD had gone, the skates were put away, two men were cleaning the floor, wan bursts of talk punctuating the sleepy swish of their long-handled brooms. The cashier, the snack bar attendant, and the pimpled boy had gone. Tuck's face still stung from the cold-water scrubbing he had given it to remove Lily's make-up.

Pete Degley laid the bills on the battered old roll-top desk in the box of room that was his office. They were new ten-dollar bills—ten of them. Tuck had never seen one hundred dollars before and his eyes seemed glued to them in wonder. He felt this to be unseemly and tried to look elsewhere—at the leather couch, as worn as the desk, where Lily sat in her slacks and jacket, a green scarf tied over her hair. At anything but the bills on the desk. It was the first time he had ever been inside the office; he had never thought of its having anything to do with him.

"This do for a starter?" Pete said round the toothpick in his mouth.

Tuck's hands hung, numb and heavy, at his sides. Pete nudged the pile. "Ain't it satisfactory?" Tuck's face burned.

"It—It's not that, Mr. Degley. You know it's not that. I—" His voice died. How could he tell Pete Degley that what he had given him already was more than the money—much more? That he, Tuck, was the indebted one, the one beholden?

"Well, put it in your jeans then, son." Pete yawned noisily. "Me, I'm beat. Guess the three of us could do with a night's sleep." He looked at Tuck and something in his eyes, tired but still bright and warm, made Tuck know that he didn't have to be told. Not Mr. Degley; he was a master hand at understanding—without being told. "I don't mind saying I was right proud of you tonight. You'll be a real skater before I get done with you, you keep on working like you have. Reckon we're in business, now." He chuckled. "That crowd was crazy for you. Thought I'd have to carry out some of them screeching girls at the end of the number. Small town boy makes good, heh heh. Tucker Holland, you'll have to beat those girls off with a club from now on in." He reached for his jacket. "Me, I got to take my girl home. See you tomorrow, Faraday. Two-thirty. I'm looking for a pretty good crowd at the afternoon session."

"Yes, sir. Thanks, Mr. Degley." Tuck pushed the bills into his pocket, still shamefaced. "Night, Mr. Degley—Pete. Night, Lily."

The trees had stopped dripping and when Tuck came out of the orchard and looked up he saw a sprinkle of stars between the white clouds that drifted ahead of the wind.

He pushed the kitchen door creakingly inward. In the darkness he caught the sound of rough breathing and reached for the fly-spotted cord. Harsh light filled the kitchen and Tuck saw his father sitting at the end of the table. Staring at the cracked oilcloth, Myron said, "I thought you wasn't coming home."

Without meaning to, Tuck moved his hand to the pocket of his jeans.

"Where else would I g-go, Pa?"

His father still did not look at him. "Off. With that feller and that girl."

Tuck laid the roll of bills on the table. He said, eagerly, "Count it, Pa." But his father only stared at the money, his veined hands lying loose in front of him. Tuck had never seen him look so tired or so old. There was something else, too, in the dejected slump of the thin shoulders. Grief? Because he had thought Tuck would not be coming home?

"The others," Myron said, as if bound to unburden his mind of what lay upon it, "they waited up to see you—to tell you. Karen said she knew all along it was going to happen. Maybe she made it up—you know kids and she's half sick with her cold. Ida put her to bed and rubbed her with that croup salve she swears by. Tom and Clete had them girls to see home, I reckon." He rubbed a thumb over a break in the oilcloth.

Tuck leaned across the table and the room seemed to sway as fatigue descended suddenly upon him. His father had waited up. Blurrily, Tuck saw him slowly part the bills, his fingers shaking. His face was gray when he looked up.

"A hundred dollars. All that money for prancin'

around a skating rink with a girl?" He shook his head, unbelieving.

"Take it," Tuck said on a long sigh.

"It's yore money," his father protested, embarrassed. "You earned it honest, I reckon."

"There'll be more. Mr. Degley—he's hired me to help with skating lessons, Saturday mornings. I—I'll be working regular at the rink."

"Working." Myron shook his head. "They call that working."

Struggling with his own sudden embarrassment, Tuck scarcely heard him. "Pa—Burl Wilson's got a kitchen stove at his place. Electric. It's in pretty fair s-shape, I reckon. You get it. M-Ma wants one bad. This one—it—it's pink."

"A pink cook stove." Myron's faded eyes, coming slowly from the bills to study Tuck's face, were uncomprehending.

"Yeah, a pink cook stove," Tuck said so loudly he was afraid he'd wakened Ida. "They make them that way now. Well, I'd be p-proud if you'd use some of the money I made tonight for it. Don't t-tell her that, just get it. Like it was your idea." Hot as his face was, he kept commanding eyes on his father. Myron's look fell.

"If that's what you want."

"It's what I w-want." Tuck picked one of the bills from the table. "I need me some shoes, too," he said. "You keep the rest."

He was halfway across the room when his father called to him and he turned to see Myron drawing himself erect, tears creeping through the stubble on his lean cheeks. "I hear how much better you talk. Good as anybody, might' near. I always said you could if you was of a mind to, but still—it's kind of a miracle, seems like."

Tuck was silent, feeling an immense weariness and a wisdom he could not share with his father.

"I 'preciate the money," Myron brought out with difficulty. "Tom or Clete wouldn't of give up a dollar if it was theirs. Not without the law made them." Bitterness cracked his voice. "But you're not like them, Tuck. You never was like them."

"Good night, Pa." Tuck steadied himself against the door frame. He couldn't remember ever having said good night to his father before; the Faradays did not bother with such niceties.

"Good night, son," his father said.

Tuck undressed quickly in the dark. He fumbled in the pocket of the jeans he had just taken off, extracted the ten-dollar bill and pushed it under his pillow. A good pair of shoes like Mr. Degley's would last a long time because he would be riding the bus to school. Maybe he was crazy. He had looked forward to quitting school. But with everything different he might as well change that, too. He heard his father's slow steps taking him to the room where Ida lay snoring, heard his shoes, one and then the other, hit the floor.

Tuck pulled the covers over his throbbing body. His head swam with weariness, but he saw a little way beyond tonight. Only a little way, but it was enough. He had needed only the straggling path through the orchard to take him to the rink. Thoughts drifted through his head, random, unimportant thoughts, pleasing because they did not disturb him. Yesterday, they had, but that was yesterday and now was now.

He thought of his brother Tom and Tolly Mayhew, of Pete and Lily at the Dixie Belle Motel, of Cletus and Elva Grimes. He smiled and the smile relaxed his face and his throat where the old cramp used to grip. He could smile at them all—even at Tuck the dummy, who had slipped into the past with all his grief. He let his breath out in a long, gentle sigh and felt his lids sinking, all of him sinking without terror or dread into sleep.